CW01431071

Knotted by The Pack

Howl's Edge Island: Omega For The Pack (Book 6)

Layla Sparks

Sapphire Ink Publishing LLC

Contents

Content Guide

If you don't have any triggers, please skip this page to avoid any spoilers! For any questions, please email author_laylasparks@yahoo.com

~ Rape (non-glorified, mentioned throughout the book but happens in the prologue)

~ Pregnancy and Birth (throughout second half of the book)

~ Group Play

~ Claiming bites

~ Backdoor Play (anal)

~ Double Penetration

Things to Know...

Omegaverse Terms

A few things to know regarding the omegaverse world. The people in the omegaverse display a more canine or wolflike behavior. Some books involve shifting into wolves. This series will have minimal shifting.

Here are some terms that will be helpful to know (*note: these definitions pertain to my stories):

Omega: A female or male who would often have multiple partners to help them during heats. Usually has a particular scent that alphas find very appealing and unable to resist.

Beta: Like a normal human, but in the wolf world

Alpha: Top of the food chain, and they gravitate to omegas. They also have a scent to attract omegas.

Delta: Ferocious and deadly. Mostly guards in my world.

Slick: Secretion from the privates. Can occur in both the pussy and the anus for an omega.

Heat: A period where an omega needs to mate - akin to ovulating in human females.

Knot: When an alpha mates and omega, and the base of the penis swells, locking the alpha and omega in place.

Rut: Alphas can go into rut phase, similar to heat. Sometimes an omega's heat will bring it on.

Scent blockers: Can come in pills or as a cream. Blocks an omega scent from attracting alphas.

Heat Suppressants: Stops an omega from going into heat

Prologue

Alana

My hands trembled as I pierced the marshmallow under the watchful eye of my crush.

Lionel was my only friend on this overnight campfire trip with fellow high schoolers. The fire crackled, illuminating the little campsite on the beach. The girls and guys were flirting shamelessly around us. Some teens were screaming and running around after we listened to a few ghost stories.

"Mind if I take care of that for you?" asked Lio, looking inquisitively at the squished marshmallow and my sticky fingers.

My heart skipped a beat at the unexpected request, but I managed to nod and passed him the stick with a smile tugging at my lips. His fingers brushed mine briefly, sending an electric jolt through me. Even though our mothers were best friends, I always felt a little nervous around Lio growing up. Recently, I'd been feeling more towards him as his inner alpha wolf emerged, signaling me with his scent, and I began perfuming as an omega at puberty. It was getting harder to control ourselves around each other. Little sly glances, winks, and smiles during our entire last year of high school made me nervous.

"You do it so well," I complimented as I watched him. I noticed his chest puffing with pride from my praise, and my inner omega rejoiced at giving him that praise. I wondered if he would kiss me tonight for the first time in our tent.

He held the marshmallow above the flames, and I watched as he expertly rotated it, the fire casting a warm glow on his face. It was mesmerizing seeing him focused on such a simple task.

"Here you go," he said, handing the stick to me, and I blew the top of it.

"Thank you," I said.

With a small smile, I inhaled the marshmallow, savoring the moment. As I bit into the warm, gooey treat, a burst of sweetness enveloped my taste buds. I closed my eyes momentarily, relishing the flavors dancing on my tongue.

When I opened my eyes, Lio was watching me intently, a soft smile playing on his lips.

"It's amazing," I said, unable to hide the delight in my voice.

He chuckled, his eyes twinkling. "I'm glad you like it. How about I set up our tent now?"

"Sure," I said, nodding while my heart tremored in my chest.

I sat at the fire alone, watching the rowdy teens pair off or hang out in groups. I could see the shadows in one tent of a couple already getting it on, and I quickly turned away, my face hot. I was still a virgin, and I hoped Lio didn't have any weird ideas up his sleeve once I was in that tent with him. I don't think he was even aware of my intense feelings for him. Music was blaring, and teen boys were smashing beer bottles on the rocks for fun.

I decided I needed to walk away for a little bit.

Dropping the stick into the campfire, I walked away from the campsite and headed towards a more secluded area surrounded by large rocks. The farther I walked, the more peace and calm came over me from the quiet. I wasn't wearing any shoes, so the sand rubbed between my toes. I wore a simple green dress that flared from my waist, stopping just above my knees. I took forever trying to find something to wear today until my twin brother, Adam, got suspicious.

As I sat on a boulder, I stared out at the ocean. Water splashed on my feet as I leaned back, watching the waves.

But the roar of the ocean waves disguised the sounds of the guys who'd followed me. I didn't know anyone had followed me until I felt a tap on my shoulder. I spun around, seeing three teenage boys who had snuck up behind me.

"Yes?" I said, my voice pleasant as I sat back down on the boulder.

"An omega like you shouldn't be alone," one of the boys leered at me, coming close to me. I could tell he was a beta. It was by the way his shoulders slumped and as the smallest of the pack. He had a pointy chin and beady eyes.

I tried to get up from the rock, but his other two friends surrounded me on both sides.

"What are you doing?" I asked, my eyes darting everywhere. Looking for an escape route. My heart was pounding hard, and my body was screaming that I was in a dangerous situation. "Do you need anything?"

"I heard omegas are sluts," cackled one of the boys, his hand on my thighs. One of the other boys began pulling my dress up.

"Stop, please," I begged, but they continued to tug at my clothes,

6

exposing me to them. My heart sank. My stomach clenched in fear. I tried to hop off the rock and run, but they pinned me down onto the boulder, spreading my legs. "Stop!"

I opened my mouth to scream, but someone's palm covered my mouth, pressing my head against the hard rock. I wiggled and squirmed, trying to get away, but I was no match for three males.

This was it. This was the day I was going to die.

I would be in the papers tomorrow. Just another omega raped or kidnapped. I tried biting his hand over my mouth but to no avail. They had already removed my underwear. I felt like I was living an out-of-body experience as I shut my eyes tight.

"Don't worry. It'll be over before you know it," said one of the guys.

"Hell no, I'm taking my sweet time," said another guy who was already violating me. A sharp rush of pain as they broke my virginity.

I tried to concentrate on the ocean waves instead.

My first time wasn't supposed to be like this. It was supposed to be with Lio. At the thought of him, tears pricked my eyes.

*Please, come look for me...*I prayed in my head over and over.

When the first guy was done, I braced myself for the next. I was numb to it all by now. Not paying attention to my body screaming for help. Then I heard a sharp hiss coming from behind me.

The hand released my mouth, and the boys instantly stepped away from me, their eyes wide at something behind me. Opening my eyes, I quickly turned to see what had scared them. A tall male stood there at my shoulder, staring daggers at the boys. He didn't have a scent and wore a loincloth.

His red bloodshot eyes stood out to me, confusing me. I'd never seen such a creature before. He wasn't one of us. My pulse was racing as I stared at him. When he bared his large sharp fangs, the boys screamed, running away from me like the devil was after them.

I didn't dare move, and I didn't dare breathe.

He was just inches from me.

Once he was satisfied they were far enough away from me, he gave me one last look and disappeared between the rocks in one lightning move. I couldn't believe what I had just seen.

I hobbled off the boulder on weak legs. My hands were shaking as I yanked my underwear back on. My innocence was over, and my life changed in just one night. It was impossible for me to go back to Lio and act like nothing happened.

I couldn't do it. And I would never tell a soul.

Chapter 1

❀

Five Years Later
Alana

"Ooh, this one's cute," an omega said to her friend as she perused the shelf of trinkets in my shop.

It had been a long, busy Friday, and these were the last of my customers for the evening. I was quietly eavesdropping as I organized a row of candles by color on the other side of my shop. I sold omega nesting supplies and named my shop *Omega Oasis* to the excitement of my grandma, who helped me run it.

I walked to the back, where Grandma was re-folding the quilts that had been rummaged through all day. She wore a blue bandana around her forehead, her white hair tied into a neat bun. She had on a blue dress with short sleeves that showed her wrinkly frail arms.

"Almost done there, Grandma?" I asked, watching her carefully fold the last quilt and place it with shaking hands on the shelf.

Grandpa had died two years ago, and after his passing, she threw herself into my shop, helping out whenever she could. At Grandpa's funeral, I'd never seen my mother cry as much as she did that day with

9

my fathers comforting her. My mother was closer to Grandpa than her own mom, and I understood why. Grandma was pretty strict as opposed to my Grandpa, who made everyone smile and have a good time. My heart ached thinking about him.

"Yes, I think so," she said, looking at her handiwork. "I just need to sweep up the backroom here. You go on ahead and ring up those girls at the front, dear."

"Alright, sounds good," I said.

I heard the little bell at the front counter and headed over there to ring up the customers.

"You have so many cute trinkets," sighed one of them, staring at the shelf with the glass wolf-shaped figurines. "I wish I could buy them all."

"Ah, it's our most popular pieces," I laughed, ringing up a small teacup with a picture of a fang on the front, a keychain, and three perfumes. "Did you find everything okay today?"

"We did," said the second omega.

"Good to hear," I said, handing them their bag after wrapping everything up in paper.

"Thank you!" said the omega, taking the bag and heading out with her friend. The door let out a small chime when they walked out of the shop. As I wiped down the pink countertop with wipes, I heard the door chime again.

Oh, did they forget something?

"Hello," said a male voice, and I looked up. *Shit, it was Lio.* And he held a pile of quilts in his hand that his mother usually sent over. He came a day early, and I usually avoided him at all costs, letting him deal with my grandmother for Saturday deliveries when I was out in the mornings.

His black hair was gelled and curled to one side, his handsome face crinkled with his soft smile, and his green eyes sparkled as he looked at me. He had only gotten better looking with age.

"Hey," I said in a crisp voice, watching as he set the pile of neatly folded quilts on the counter. "Thank you for the delivery."

"Glad I finally get to see you," said Lio, his teeth stark white. He wore faded jeans with the biggest belt buckle and a tight white shirt two sizes too small for him.

"Yeah, I'm usually super busy," I said, leaning back against the counter.

Alright, he gave me the quilts. He could go now.

But of course, he didn't get the message. He continuously wanted to hang out or be in my presence, but I'd text him a bullshit excuse for not making it. After the fateful night on the beach, I didn't tell a soul about what happened.

Not even him.

After that night, I ran all the way home and cried all night in my bed. All my feelings for him had dwindled. It was no longer something magical for me. From then on, I limited interactions with him and distanced myself from all males who weren't my family.

"Me too," said Lio, who seemed intent on having small talk with me.

I swallowed when he crossed his arms and leaned over on the counter, watching me.

"Well, how's work?" I asked.

"Very knotty," he chuckled. He worked as a professional knotter in one of the omega heat clinics on the island, a drastic change from the

11

nerdy kid he was back in school.

When I had first heard about it, I was shocked but also realized it was much easier for me not to like him in *that* way- when he was busy easing omegas during their heats and knotting them. A part of me also broke down, wishing that wasn't his job, but I had shot him down every chance. Professional knotters made a ton of money at their jobs, signing contracts that they wouldn't take a mate or otherwise lose their job. They weren't allowed to have babies either, and there were various birth control options in place now at the heat clinics.

A young, virile alpha like him was in hot demand. *Who was I to stop him?*

"Oof, sorry I asked," I said sarcastically.

"What can I do to get you to smile?" he asked, looking at me curiously. Ever since the fateful night at the camp, it wasn't easy for me to smile and be as light-hearted as I used to be.

I bit my lip, wanting him gone now.

"Sorry, it's just been a busy day," I said, breathing hard. Just then, my grandma popped her head around the corner and gracefully hugged Lio, her lilac perfume wafting past me.

"How's Mama Keera doing?" she asked.

"She's doing good," said Lio, louder than ever. "The new quilts are here for you." He was close to my family since we had grown up together, so they adored him.

"I wish she would accept payment for it," muttered my grandma, shaking her head as she softly touched the quilts. "I will call her later."

"Of course," said Lio. "Have a good day. Both of you ladies. See you at the Shadow Hunt's Fest tomorrow."

He nodded at me, concern in his eyes. Then he gave Grandma

one more hug and left the shop. I breathed out a sigh of relief. Every time I saw him, it was like a wave of anxiety would rush through me. Uncertainty and fear even though he had done nothing to me. I wanted to avoid everything from my past.

Including him.

Chapter 2

Alana

The sun warmed my skin as I curled my bare toes in the sand.

I enjoyed being out at the beach early Saturday mornings to relax while Grandma took care of *Omega Oasis* with her friend. I was lying on the beach towel in a remote area and wearing a black bikini and a tank top. Pulling my diary out of my rucksack, I opened it and watched the waves as I held the pen between my fingers. I scanned the horizon with my eyes, looking and searching.

Always searching for him. For the creature who saved me.

I never saw him again after that traumatizing night. It felt like I had been dreaming the entire time and that it was just a nightmare. Did I really see a creature I'd never seen before? I couldn't comprehend it, and I wanted answers. He literally appeared out of nowhere, and I was starting to doubt myself and think it was a figment of my imagination.

The night I was attacked, I had gone home and cried for hours in my room. Over the months, I couldn't shake off the resentment and rage that I felt at everyone around me, especially my parents.

"What's wrong with you, Lana?" my mother, Tiana, huffed when

I barely talked to her or my dads for the third day in a row after the attack.

"Nothing," I said, looking away in case she could read me. No one was allowed to know my shame. "Why are you always trying to control everything I do?"

Sadness filled her eyes as she calmly sat on my bed beside me.

"Did something happen? What can I do to make it better?"

"Nothing," I said, heading to the closet and throwing my things into a suitcase. "I'm moving out."

"What?" she asked, dumbfounded as she watched me. My heart ached, and my stomach hurt. I couldn't bear to be home in this happy family who thought everything was hunky dory, and peachy. They wouldn't want an unclean girl like me living here. "Where are you going to live then?"

"With Grandma," I muttered.

"Oh, okay," she said, and I could hear the relief in her voice. Grandma only lived a block away. "Well, when you feel better, I would love for you to come back home. We all love you. Your siblings, fathers, and I are going to miss you."

And that's how I ended up living with my grandparents until I finished college and opened my shop with Papa Grant's assistance. I still lived with them, but my siblings always visited me like nothing had changed. If I spent too much time with my mother, she would get me to open up about everything. And ever since I moved out, our relationship had never been the same. I don't think I'll ever have the courage to tell my family what happened to me.

I rummaged through my rucksack, looking for my binoculars which were underneath the pepper spray I carried everywhere. I usually scanned the beach with binoculars while no one was there. If people saw me, they'd think I was weird. But as usual, I couldn't see him anywhere. I sadly placed the binoculars back into the bag as I could see beach-goers arriving now that it was sunrise. I just wanted proof. Proof that the creature still existed. As I placed everything back into the bag, I felt goosebumps on the back of my neck.

Like someone was watching me.

I slowly turned, and seeing no one- I breathed a sigh of relief. I was getting too obsessed and freaking myself out for no reason. *Breathe Alana.*

It was sunset by the time I arrived at the annual barbeque for Shadow Hunt's Fest, which was already full of people. I eyed everyone as I stepped out of the car that I received for a birthday present from my dads. I was so conflicted about what to wear, so I opted for denim shorts with a striped tank top of blue and yellow. My hair was in a messy bun with a blue hairclip to match my tank top, complete with silver hoop earrings and white sneakers. I felt good about myself and resolved to enjoy my off day even though I was not too fond of partying.

I was the last to arrive at the park. I saw my dads and other pack alphas surrounding three grills at the front entrance of the reserved park.

"Welcome, daughter!" boomed Papa Grant, pulling me into a big hug. I hadn't seen him in a while, and his normally chiseled face was now covered in wrinkles, and his eyebrows were gray, matching his hair. He was always so happy to see me even though I moved out years ago. He never showed his disappointment at what I did. Every time I visited him, he had the biggest grin on his face like he missed his oldest daughter.

"Hey, Dad," I said, smiling when I saw the massive pile of burgers and hot dogs on a tray. "You guys have been busy."

"We're enjoying this nice weather," he boomed. "How's my little entrepreneur?"

"The shop's going good," I said, rolling my eyes with a smile.

"Here, take a plate," said my father, Tony, hugging me next. He was the father who encouraged us to delve into our dreams as kids. He played guitar to this day, entertaining the people of Howl's Edge Island. The guitar was pretty ancient, which always sat in the corner of his room, which we were never allowed to touch as kids.

"What would you like?" asked Sam, who was already grabbing me a plate and heading to the picnic table. The red bandana on his head was nearly falling off from how frantic he was managing the meats. I followed him and pointed to the various picks of barbequed meats that he picked out with a pair of tongs for me. Sam was the fun dad and the one I enjoyed being around the most. Grant was more of the disciplinarian. "Here you go, daughter. How's life been?"

"Good. Been working a lot," I answered, taking the plate from him. After conversing for a little bit about my shop and telling him Grandma was arriving here early after closing the shop for the day, I moved on to my father, Wesley, who was wincing as the hot grill smoke floated to his eyes.

"Why hello there, Lanny," he greeted me. He was the most affectionate, soft-hearted father. He hated to see me in tears and spoiled me rotten. He rubbed his hand through his blond hair- which mainly had turned white as he struggled to turn the meat on the grill.

"Are you okay there?" I asked him with a smile. Sam took over the barbeque, and Wesley breathed out a long sigh of relief.

"I hate this," he said, rolling his eyes. "I'm probably the only alpha dad in the world who hates doing barbeque. It's just so hot and messy."

I laughed, and we both stopped when we heard fireworks above us.

"Ooh, they're already starting the fireworks," I said. "I'm going to find Mom and everyone else. I'll catch up with you later."

"Sounds good."

I walked further into the park, seeing foldable chairs everywhere and people setting up blankets on the ground. I spotted my mother, Tiana, talking with her best friends, Keera and Vanessa, sitting on a large checkered blanket. Around them were plates of food their alphas brought for them.

My sisters Roxanne and Sarah were sitting on the blanket next to them.

"No, that's enough, Grant," whined Mom when he placed another hamburger next to her pile of barbequed meat. He winked at her, and she blushed. I loved that they still had such a strong affection for each other. It was the only thing that made me believe that not all relationships were horrible. But ever since my attack, I had never gone near an alpha. Never touched one and probably never will.

I sat between my mom and my sisters, balancing my plate on my lap. My sisters were deep in conversation, staring at Roxanne's phone. Roxanne was the youngest in the family at the age of seventeen, and Sarah was twenty. They were hunched deep in conversation while they looked at the phone.

"What are you looking at on the phone?" I asked, startling them.

Sarah turned to me and smiled widely. "Hey, big sis. Long time no see."

My sisters were always so excited to see me. I knew it was the hardest on them after I left, but they were grown up now.

"I know, right," I said. "So what's new?"

"Roxy thinks she captured a ghost on camera," said Sarah, squinting again at the picture.

I laughed out loud.

"Oh, come on, Roxy. There's no such thing," I said, and she looked at me with wide brown eyes. Her hair was in braids, and she wore a cute green summer dress.

"Well, *you* may not believe it," said Roxanne as I took a bite of the steaming hot dog.

"I'm sure it was a blur on the photo or something," I said, chuckling. Roxy was always the most imaginative sibling and believed in all the conspiracy theories surrounding Howl's Edge, like one day omegas would be rounded up in the new construction buildings and even crazier theories of a giant living in the woods.

I munched on the food while I watched people setting up the fireworks. My mother was chattering away with her friends, and it took her about five minutes to notice I was there.

"Alana," she said, startled when she noticed I was sitting beside her. She wrapped one arm around me, hugging me. "How are you, my dear?"

"Good," I said. "Hey, Auntie Keera and Vanessa."

We talked for a little bit about my business which was always the hot

19

topic of conversation, the weather, and if I had found an alpha pack yet to marry, which I quickly dismissed by changing the subject. Getting up to throw away my empty plate, I walked over to the trashcan- taking a break from all the meet-ups. It was pretty hot out, and the back of my neck was sweating.

"Nice to see you're here, Lana," said a deep male voice from behind. Only one person called me that. I spun around, seeing Lio standing there with his thumbs tucked into his belt.

"Yep, I'm here," I said.

"It's the second day in a row that I've gotten to see you. How did I get so lucky?"

"Yeah, we usually see each other once every couple of years," I said dryly, stepping around him to head back toward my family. But he stopped me with a touch to my arm. I stood frozen in place, feeling the warmth of his fingers press against my arm.

He tensed, sensing the change in my mood.

My omega pineapple perfume thickened in the air, and he immediately released me with a frown on his face. I knew he could sense my sudden mood. All day at his knotting job, he was supposed to read omega emotions and calm them through their heat.

"Everything okay?" he asked me with concern in his eyes. I suddenly felt silly. He wasn't a threat or danger to me at all. I needed to get a grip on myself.

"Yes, of course," I said.

"Watch fireworks with me?" he asked, deciding not to interrogate me further. "We can go on top of my car."

"I...sure," I said, walking with him. I felt guilty about being afraid of his touch, so I quickly agreed. It wasn't like me to be so terrified so quickly -but I hadn't felt an alpha's touch like that. And the only touch I ever felt wasn't good at all.

Chapter 3

Lio

While we lay on top of the hood of my car, I looked over at Alana. She was staring at the sky, lit with different colors from the fireworks. She looked lost in her thoughts with her hands behind her head. I was lying next to her, one knee pulled up with my hand resting on it. I picked at the threads of my jeans ripping at the knees as I looked at her.

She was beautiful.

The way her hair fell in soft waves around her face, and her skin glowed under the lights, made me catch my breath. She had always been beautiful to me, and I always had dreamt that one day she would be the omega of my pack. In my heart, I thought she was my fated mate.

But those were dreams long forgotten. Dreams I had years ago until she distanced herself from me and all our friends after high school.

And that's when I gave up all hope of ever having an omega. I've decided to pursue an unorthodox career that guaranteed an omega would never want to join my pack. My job as a professional knotter ensured I would be lonely in my personal life. Sex had turned into a chore. Something that only happened at work. Every day, after I went home after work, the loneliness hit me like a ton of bricks. It didn't matter how expensive my home or my car was. There was always that need.

For years I would end up laying in a dark bedroom alone for nights on end and craving an omega to cuddle with. An omega that I could call my own. If Alana told me to quit my job right now and she wanted to be with me, I would do it in a heartbeat. Only for her.

But she hadn't shown interest in me since the campfire night and completely refused to talk to me about it.

"I like the red," she said, snapping me out of my thoughts.

My gaze turned to the sky. "The red fireworks, you mean?"

"Yes, and the silver just goes with it," she muttered, mesmerized by the lights. Even when we were children, she had always loved fireworks. And I loved to experience it with her and watch her face glow with happiness. It was the only time I'd see her let down her guard. But now, she was a fully grown woman lying next to me on the hood of my car, and she was breathtaking.

"I agree," I said, watching the lights crackle in the sky and the resounding boom that followed. "How have you been lately? I mean, *really* been."

"Just taking care of the shop, you know," she said. She always had that guard up. Talking about her business and never about herself. "How about you?"

"I've been struggling lately," I said, and she turned her head away from the fireworks, looking at me curiously. It had been a while since she looked at me with interest like that, and my heart thumped as our eyes locked.

"Why are you struggling?"

"I still want a mate, you know? An omega to have and a full pack of my own to cherish her too," I said, opening up. Maybe if I was open more, I'd get her to talk more about herself. I wanted to know what made her tick these days. I knew for sure she wasn't mated either.

"But don't you see omegas daily? Like knot them too?" she asked, biting her lip while her face turned pink.

"That's rutting for me," I explained. "There's no love, like, or even any sort of attachment there. But with you...I feel some of that."

There. I fucking said it.

I watched her expression carefully as she started breathing harder. She sat up, breaking eye contact with me. I got up and placed my hand over hers on her lap. Her hand started trembling under mine.

"I'm sorry, I'm just..." she started to say. Her scent began to rise with worry, tension, and...fear. *Why the hell was she scared of me?* Unless there was something...because I'd never had an omega be fearful of me. My job was to keep them calm.

"What is it, Lana?" I asked, using the pet name that I used to call her.

"I can't," she said, ripping her hand from mine and jumping off the hood of the car. She rubbed her palms on her shorts, looking regretfully at me. "I'll see you later, okay?"

"Please, you can tell me anything. What's bothering you?"

"No," she said finally. "There's nothing to tell."

I watched her walk away, her hair swinging down her back in her hurry to get away from me. I was starting to sense that something happened to this omega.

24

Something bad.

Chapter 4

Alana

I took deep breaths in the car as I drove away from the park. My nerves were jittery around Lio, and I couldn't take any chances being alone with him. I pushed him away several times over the years, and I missed him, but it would be too awkward to act like nothing happened. A dull heartache settled in my chest, wondering if he would ever give up everything for me. To give up his well-paying profession and his luxurious life. He was so work-oriented I didn't believe he would ever do that.

And there was no way I would be the side omega after his day of rutting at work.

Parking my car at the beach, I craved a few moments to myself before going to my grandma's house. As I strolled around the beach, I decided to go to the area where I was attacked. I couldn't allow my past to control me anymore and stop me from living my life. I wanted a loving and happy relationship with a pack, just like any omega desired to be.

The boulder was still there. The one they laid me onto. The sight of it sent chills down my spine.

I avoided the beach at night at all costs after the attack. Memories rushed through me as I placed my hand on the cold granite rock. I listened to the sounds of the ocean crashing against the shore. Quickly turning away from the rock, I looked at the area where I'd seen the creature who had saved me. I walked around the area and stopped in front of a huge bed of rocks that was like a wall towering above me. In between the rocks was a small entrance that looked like it led to a cave.

Hunched over, I walked inside the dark cave, turning on the flashlight on my phone. There was nothing but puddles inside, and it creeped me out. *What if the creature lived in here?* I decided I needed to get the hell out of there.

But as I turned to leave, I saw an opening on the other side. My curiosity getting the better of me, I continued walking down the cave and came upon another entrance. It smelled so dewy and gross in here. I went to the end of the cave and peeked through the opening on the other side. My jaw fell open at what I saw.

It was like an entire secret city on this side.

I stood there in awe. There were two giant walls of rocks on either side of me that expanded into another horizon if I continued to walk down this road. I could barely see anything in the night as I shined my flashlight around wildly.

Suddenly I felt a hand clamp over my mouth.

"Stop right there," said a deep voice.

I struggled against him, trying to step on him and punch him with my elbow. He was like a brick wall as I flailed with panic. He started walking me down the pathway leading to an open area with people roaming about in this secret city. It was dark, but I could make out the figures of tall, slender people walking around in nothing but rags.

The hand on my mouth was ice-cold. He didn't have a smell or a scent to him either. He released my mouth, and I quickly spun around.

My stomach dropped when I realized he was the same creature I had seen the night I was attacked.

The one and only.

I screamed, trying to run, but he had a firm grasp on my wrist. I opened my eyes to see myself surrounded by ten more of his kind. Cold, pale skin and glowing red eyes in the dark as they leaned in towards me. My screams were attracting more of them to me, like an infestation, and I immediately stopped.

They were here to kill me.

"What the fuck?! Get away," I screamed, plastering myself against the guy holding my wrist. But instead, they leaned towards me, smelling and sniffing me. One looked like the elder of the pack. "You're not werewolves."

"We're vampires," he said, and my eyes widened. My worst fears and suspicions came true. I knew I'd seen a vampire the night I was attacked, but I refused to believe until I'd seen him again. They weren't supposed to exist. Vampires belonged in the fairy tales that teachers read to us in school. They were bloodsuckers of the worst kind, preying especially on omegas, who they deemed precious blood.

The elderly vampire smiled, his yellow fangs visible under the moonlight. He sniffed my neck, and I shuddered. Flashbacks of my attack spun in my brain, and my body went into fight-or-flight mode. My heart leaped in my throat, until the younger man who brought me here stopped him.

"Volgriff, no need for that," he said, pulling me behind him.

Did he want me instead for himself? I thought wildly.

My breathing was erratic, and my pulse was pounding so hard I thought I might faint. They were actual vampires. They had no scent, had fangs, and their eyes were red of various shades. I focused my gaze on the ground, gripping my phone in my pocket. My phone was the only thing I had on me right now. I didn't dare dial for help while they watched me closely.

"Move out of the way, young buck," growled the elder. "We can all have a drink and then dispose of her in the ocean. It's Shadow Hunt's Fest, and she was just celebrating with her people. The day they massacred thousands of our kind."

I didn't know Shadow Hunt's Fest was about that. Growing up, I learned that it was just a celebration of our independence. I shut my eyes, taking a couple of deep breaths. They were ready to kill me. To drink my blood and dispose of my body. No one would ever find me.

"Let us wait until the full moon," said the younger vampire. I kept my eyes trained on the sandy ground, away from the leering creatures. "It's only a couple of days away, and I can keep her until then. I'll make sure she doesn't go back to her people."

"Hmm, don't let her escape," said Volgriff. "And the magic in her blood will be more powerful under the full moon."

"I'll make sure she doesn't escape. You know you can trust me."

The elderly one sighed. "You have a point there, James. Keep her until then. Everyone step away from the omega."

I didn't breathe until they all stepped away from me, breaking the circle around me. When they finally left, I let out a long breath. But now, I was trapped with this vampire, who wasn't any less dangerous than the others.

James gruffly pulled me along, walking me across the small city. I saw betas crawling on the sand or sitting on rocks with blood running down their necks with vacant expressions on their faces. Like they didn't know why they were there. They didn't even look at me as I passed by them.

"Oh god," I muttered under my breath. I was soon going to be one of them.

We walked towards a small hut that was standing on sturdy wooden stilts. The roof was thatched with straw that fluttered from the night breeze. The entrance was marked with a rotting wood door.

He silently took me into the small hut, which was lit up by a single candle on a wooden table. The walls had wooden planks which looked like it could collapse at any time, and cobwebs decorated the corners. In the middle of the hut was a straw mattress covered in sheets. I took in the small hut in one sweep of my gaze. I tried remembering my steps back to the secret cave to get back home, but we had gone in so many circles, and it was going to be impossible unless I traced my footsteps in the sand, which would disappear by now.

"You will sleep here," he said, pointing to the bare ground in the living room.

"But there's nothing there," I said, staring at the uneven patches of dried mud. Then he grabbed a blanket from his bed and set it on the floor. I felt queasy and strangely aroused that I would be sleeping in something he used. He grabbed a rope from the corner of the hut and bent down at my feet, tying one end around my ankle. His long hair brushed against my thighs as he worked, muttering to himself like a crazy person. His nearness and touch put my nerves on high alert, turning me on at the same time. I was confused about my body's reaction to him.

"There," he said, tugging on the rope, tightening it around my ankle. "I'll show you where the shower is and where you will use the bathroom."

James grabbed my hand again with his cold one, guiding me outside of his hut as I analyzed my surroundings to escape. Grandma was expecting me home, and I hated the fact that she was probably worried about me right now. The shower in the back was a bucket on the roof that he pulled with a chain to release water. There was a small ground stove outside for cooking. There wasn't a sink, just barrels of ocean water outside the home.

"Please just let me go," I said to him as he led me inside again.

"That's impossible," he said, laying two blankets on the ground for me. "You will tell your people about us. We've lived here peacefully for many years. I don't have a choice."

"I won't, I promise," I said ardently, kneeling on the blanket. I had never begged for my life before, but this warranted that I had to. I was going to die out here and needed to do anything possible to get back home. I was dizzy from lack of sleep, and it had to be well late into the night.

He sat on a wooden chair, observing me with hooded eyes. He was tall and slender, wearing only a loincloth around his thighs. The vampires here didn't have much, and I could see that. His chest muscles bulged every time he moved, and I tried not to stare at him even though I was scared for my life.

"Your people have persecuted ours for years," he said. "There's no chance I will allow you to return."

He got up to leave.

31

"Why did you save me then?!" I shouted when he was about to step out of the hut. "The night I was attacked."

Chapter 5

Alana

He stopped and turned around slowly to gaze at me. He was quiet for a moment with a thoughtful look in his red eyes. The paleness of his skin made the red in his eyes and the darkness of his hair more vivid.

"I'll be back," he said gruffly- ignoring my question. *Which meant he remembered who I was...*

I watched as he left the hut, and I was more confused than ever. Why was I here if he was willing to save me that night? I suddenly remembered the phone I was clutching in my hand with the flashlight still on. They must not have seen my phone, and if they did, they probably didn't know what it was.

I gingerly sat on the blanket cross-legged, wishing I didn't wear such skimpy denim shorts. My thighs had goosebumps from the chill in the air. A nice pair of jeans or even leggings would have been better. There was no sun in this area of the island, and their chosen place was so isolated. Even if I screamed bloody murder, no one would hear me. My screams would be covered up by the sounds of the ocean, and there was a long way back through the cave system.

I noticed the battery on my phone was almost dying. I dialed for help. When the phone started ringing, my heart was in my throat the entire time. Hoping against hope he didn't come back at this moment.

Please pick up. Hurry up.

When they finally picked up, it felt like an eternity.

"Howl's Edge Protection Services," greeted the operator. "May I get your name and location, please?"

"I'm Alana, and I've been kidnapped by vampires," I whispered harshly into the phone, hoping they could hear me above the whispering. When the words left my mouth, it sounded ludicrous even to me.

"Haha, we don't do prank calls," said the operator loudly, and I could hear her comrades laughing in the background as she whispered *'vampires'* to them.

"No! This is real," I shouted.

Just then, the vampire walked into the hut, and upon seeing me talking on my phone, his eyes widened. He rushed over to me, snatching the phone from my hand.

"Hey!" I yelled, running after him as he walked outside with my phone. He hurled it against a boulder, and the phone smashed into a million pieces before me. My heart sank, and my hopes dashed. *That was it.* My last line of escape. The other vampires lingering around stared at us as I screamed at him. "You didn't need to do that! You're such a fucking monster."

I dashed back inside, away from the other vampires' prying eyes, my eyes burning with impending tears as James came inside after me.

"You should never have done that," he said, his eyes hard as he sat on the edge of his straw bed. "I will hand you over right now to Volgriff if you keep acting like this."

"You wouldn't," I said, out of breath and sitting on the blanket again. The hard floor was hurting my bottom, and I wished I was at home on my soft, cozy bed at my grandparents'. A wave of homesickness washed over me.

"What makes you so sure?" he asked.

"You saved me that night from my attackers," I said. "That's why I'm so sure."

"It's only because I hate your kind," he said with a disgusted curl to his lips. "Don't think you're so special, sweetheart."

I bit my lip with uncertainty now.

"Well, I hate vampires," I retorted. "Gross, blood-sucking creatures."

"You werewolves think you're perfect, huh?" he said. "How disgusting is it that alphas share one female? I would never share my female with anyone. Ever."

Rage boiled within me at his insult.

"It's normal for an omega to have more than one mate," I said. "She needs it to survive during her heats. It may seem weird to you, but it's completely normal to us."

"Then it's normal for vampires to feed on their natural prey," he countered. "Your people are arrogant."

"We're not."

"Really?"

"Well, *I'm* not," I said, now realizing how volatile my situation was. He could toss me to the vampires at any moment. "I don't care that you drink blood to survive. I just don't want it to be me."

"Get some sleep," he said, gruffly nodding to my makeshift bed on the floor next to his straw mattress. And that was the end of that.

I didn't want to talk to him anymore as I lay on the ground, trying to get comfortable. But this was feeding time for the vampires, and it was hard to fall asleep. I closed my eyes, listening to the betas cry out when they were bitten and the murmur from the vampires, followed by slurping sounds. My stomach twisted and turned as I fell into a restless sleep.

I opened my eyes to see myself surrounded. Four pale vampires surrounded me, crouched over my body. Red eyes shone with excitement as they stared at my naked body.

"I want her juicy thighs."

One of them leaned down to my thigh, cold breath grazing across my skin before puncturing my skin with his teeth. Then they swarmed all around me, ready to bite every place on my body.

"Please stop!" I screamed.

James

"Wake up, omega," I said, gently shaking her by the shoulder. She was lost in her dream world, shaking and crying. "Omega."

She finally opened her eyes and looked at me with bloodshot eyes, tears drenching her face.

"Get away!" she screamed, scrambling away from me and backing into a corner.

"Omega," I said, softer this time. It hurt me that she was so scared of me. I would never hurt her, even though she insulted me earlier today.

36

She looked so delicate and feeble as she trembled in the corner away from me.

"My name is Alana, not Omega," she hissed, looking at me with narrowed eyes. In my heart, I knew she was ready to escape. Anything will set her off right now. But if she went out there, my people were waiting for her. It would be dangerous.

"Why are you crying?" I asked her, slowly inching towards her on my knees. I didn't want to scare her any more than she already was. The stark fear in her almond-shaped eyes was real, and I wondered what she had been dreaming about. Her long dark hair lay messily around her shoulders, revealing a beauty that had grown over the years since I saved her from the rapists.

"Please, let me go," she said, her voice breaking. "I miss my home. I have a family who will miss me."

My heart broke for her.

I wanted to take her home more than anything. But my people would cast me out, and I would have nowhere to go if I betrayed them. I knelt in front of her, not touching her - especially after what she had gone through in the past.

"I wish I could set you free," I sighed, and she looked at me with renewed hope in her eyes. "But you're safest in my home. And you need to stay here."

"So you have a heart?" she asked out of the blue.

"What kind of question is that?"

"Why don't you just feed on me and get it over with?" she asked, dropping her head to one side and moving her hair out of the way. Her beautiful golden skin glowed, her blood pulsing deliciously underneath. The scent of her was unbelievable when she was offering herself to me. My body gravitated towards her, but I stopped myself. Every moment of being alone with her in this tiny hut was dangerous.

She was temptation itself.

"No," I said gruffly, looking away from her exposed neck. "I don't feed on people."

"Oh?" she asked, her eyes widening. At least she stopped crying, and that was good. I needed to keep her distracted from her predicament, and all wasn't hopeless like she thought it was. Maybe I could negotiate with Volgriff and keep her instead as my mate.

"I only feed on wild animals," I said. The fear and emotions of the beta made their blood taste bitter and sour. But when an omega offered herself up freely, that blood was richer and sweeter than any other blood on Howl's Edge.

My nostrils flared as I tried to breathe normally, being so close to her. I swallowed when she let out a small smile.

"Then let me go," she said. "I'm useless to you, right?"

"To me, yes," I said. "But not to the others. It's not my place to take you out of here. They are trusting me with keeping you here until the full moon."

She laid a small hand on my bare thigh, and my cock hardened, barely covered with the loincloth. Her hand was small, but her touch was powerful. It sent shockwaves through my body, causing every inch of my body to awaken. My breathing quickened as I placed my hand over hers, pulling her hand off me.

"Sorry," she whispered, seeing my primal response to her touch.

I clenched my teeth to keep from pouncing on her. To feed and ravish her all for myself.

"The reason I saved you that night," I said- realizing she needed to know to feel safe. "The night you were attacked and hearing your muffled yells reminded me of the time my sister was murdered. Long ago, when the government persecuted us fifty-five years ago."

"Oh," she said, her eyes widening. Droplets of tears hung on the end of her eyelashes. "I'm so sorry to hear that."

"She was taken by five alphas that night," I said. "While they forced me to watch. It was the worst night of my life. Her screams still fucking haunt me to this day. I was her only family member left, and I was supposed to protect her."

"How did you escape?"

The memory washed over me like wildfire.

"When they ripped her head off her body, rage took me over," I said, still unable to believe what I had done that night. It was like another force had taken me over. "I killed the two alphas holding me. I cried over my sister's body that day before going into hiding. I had never cried any other day. Volgriff had found me and brought me here to this community. A safe haven for our people."

"Damn," she said, her eyes wide while I spoke. "That's so horrible. I'm sorry for what they did, but lots have changed now. Omegas used to be second-class citizens, but now we have even more rights than the average beta. God, I can't believe they did that to you and your family. I feel sick to my stomach."

She clutched her belly, and I lifted my arm as if to hug and comfort her but stopped myself. My gaze softened when I saw the sincerity in her eyes, her own memories of her attack coming to surface.

"Goodnight, Alana," I said, getting up instead. "There's nothing to worry about in my home. I will not hurt you."

She nodded gratefully, letting out a small yawn. My breathing quickened as my gaze focused on her plump lips, wishing she would take my cock into her mouth...

Fuck. I couldn't go there with her.

Chapter 6

Alana

The next morning I woke up to the sun peeking through the holes of the thatched roof.

My body was sore as hell as I slowly got off the ground. James was still sleeping on his cot, soft snores emitting from him. I looked at him more closely while he was sleeping. He looked like a sculpted statue with that body of his. His black curly hair was messy and wild, stopping short of his ears, curling over one eye.

He would have been good-looking in my book if he hadn't kidnapped me.

I needed to pee. I walked to the front door, pushing it open, and it let out a long squeak. Looking back over at James, his body was still and unmoving. He had said last night that the rope on me would be long enough to go around the back for the bathroom. I bent down, trying to untie the rope around my ankle, but he had tied it with so many loops, and I needed to use the bathroom badly.

As I walked outside, I saw that it was virtually empty. It was quiet, and I guessed the vampires were nocturnal creatures. In the back of the hut, there was a hole in the ground which he pointed out was how I was supposed to use the bathroom. There was a brick wall around it, shaped like a half moon surrounding it. It smelled, and I crinkled my nose in disgust. I didn't want to squat and pee, but I had to.

Before peeling off my shorts and panties, I looked around to see if anyone was looking. It wasn't very secluded. Anyone can come around and take a peek at me.

I quickly pulled down my shorts and underwear, squatting over the dreadful hole in the ground. It took me a few seconds to finally let go and just pee. When I finished, I walked to the makeshift shower. Maybe a quick shower would make me feel better. I was hot and sticky with sweat, so I removed my clothes, hanging them on a rope a few inches from me.

I stared at the bucket hanging precariously above me.

I hesitantly pulled on the rope to dip some water over me. When the water splashed over my body, I was relieved it was warm from the sun and not freezing cold.

I looked around for any kind of soap, and since there wasn't any, I pulled the rope again to dump the rest of the salty water over me. But instead of the water falling, the bucket itself started to fall in slow motion over my head. I screeched, and a hand immediately shot out, catching it.

I stared at the hand for a second, dumbfounded - turning to see that it was attached to James, who had woken up.

"Are you okay?" he asked, looking away from my naked body and tying the bucket back up.

"Yes, you caught that just in time," I said breathlessly. I was still in shock by how quick his reflexes were. "Were you right there the whole time?"

"When I heard you yell, that's when I came out," he explained gruffly, concentrating as he pulled the rope to hand a fresh bucket of water.

"That was fast," I said, placing a hand over my bare chest. I was completely naked, and he wasn't ashamed as he looked over at me. His eyes lingered on the dark patch between my legs. "Can't you just leave the bucket on the ground? It doesn't make sense that it's high up there."

I tried to keep talking to keep him distracted. And to keep him from looking at me like that and making my body heat up for him. Slick was already drenching my pussy as I tried to regulate my breathing. It felt so wrong feeling like this for a vampire. I had never felt this visceral powerful reaction in my body for anyone.

It was like an earthquake hit me as I gazed into his ruby-red eyes. He was taller than me. Raw and powerful. Muscular than anyone else I met. If he wanted to take me, I wouldn't have a chance.

"I like putting the bucket up there," he said softly while looking into my eyes. "It feels like old times. Like a real shower. That's why I do it."

"Oh," I said, mesmerized, still using my arm to cover my breasts. Goosebumps rose from my skin from the light wind.

"I can help you," he said quickly, realizing I was shivering.

"Do you...do you have soap?" I asked.

"I do. Sorry, I can't help but stare. Your beauty is not like the vampire women," he said, quickly going inside the hut to grab me some. He actually admitted to staring at me and called me a beauty. My skin warmed, and my heart fluttered against my better judgment.

When had I gotten so easily flattered? I had to remember that he was my captor, and he was being creepy. I had to get my act together.

When he came back with the bar of homemade soap, he poured some water over it and handed it to me.

"Thank you," I said, rubbing it between my hands and getting it sudsy. I realized he was still standing there, watching me. "I think I got this now. You can leave now."

"I can rinse you when you're finished," he offered, watching my hands. I bit my lip with hesitation. "I don't want the bucket to fall on you again."

I quickly rubbed the soap over my arms, making sure it got soapy enough. Then, I pretended he wasn't there as I started to wash my breasts, rubbing soap all over. I heard harsh breathing and saw James watching me with his loincloth stretched by his cock. *Oh fuck*. He was getting turned on the more I washed my breasts. I was also horny, and I couldn't help but rub my nipples next with the bar of soap in circles. He licked his lips as I rubbed my belly and abdomen next with soap, rubbing all around until my body was covered in white bubbles.

I was too shy to wash my privates next in front of him.

"You can rinse me now," I said to him.

"You didn't finish," he said. "Go ahead." He was looking at me between my legs, nodding towards it.

My pussy clenched at his words. I was breathing hard when I rubbed the soap against the palm of my hand to make it soapy. I hesitantly spread my legs a couple of inches apart.

"Wider," he said huskily.

I swallowed, spreading my legs further apart as I stood there with soap dripping off my body. Then I brought my hand down between my legs, rubbing all around my pussy. I could see the hint of his hard cock showing through the loincloth, hard for me. This was sensual and different for me. Nothing like my brutal attack years ago. This feeling made me want to pounce on him. But my heart pounded fast at the thought. I wasn't sure if it was fear or arousal.

I slowly rubbed my folds with soap, my breathing and scent thickening. I looked at him with hooded eyes, trembling the more I rubbed my fingers around my pussy and my clit.

"Keep going," he ordered. "We need you shiny and clean."

My pulse rate increased, and my belly clenched the more I rubbed. This was way different than touching myself in the bedroom at night. With this vampire watching me, it was a completely different feeling instead. Hotter and wilder.

I rubbed harder over my clit, and I moaned as currents went through my pussy. I pressed down harder, rubbing in circles until my legs shook and trembled under his watchful gaze. Breathing hard, I released my sensitive clit looking up at him. His nostrils were flared, and he looked like he was ready to eat me.

"Can you rinse me now?" I asked.

"I will," he said. "While I do that, you must wash your ass next."

"Okay," I whispered, my pussy clenching repeatedly from my orgasm. He held the bucket as he poured the water over me. It felt good to finally get clean.

"Turn, so I can pour the water over you," he said. I turned around, my back facing him as he poured the water over my back. "Bend down and wash yourself, omega."

Heart beating fast in my throat, I turned around and bent down as he ordered. It felt like a dream like he was compelling me to obey. I did this mindlessly, but I wanted to follow his orders and please him.

To display everything to him.

I was confused by what I was feeling. This should only happen with alphas. While James poured water over my bottom, I shyly dipped my finger between my cheeks, washing up and down.

Before I could scramble back up and be done with our little game, he had another request.

"Hold yourself open for me so I pour the water in between," he said.

Oh my god.

I could barely breathe as I spread my ass cheeks open for him. I felt the trickle of water go down my crack, and then a huge gush of water hit my anus, and I nearly fell back in pleasure.

"Yes, right there," I gasped out loud. Then he stopped pouring water. "Oh, never mind."

I straightened back up, embarrassed at staying bent over waiting for more. My pussy was still clenching from my orgasm.

"Thank you for helping me."

"You're welcome," he said as I turned to grab my clothing. "Why are you in a hurry? You have nowhere to go."

"I know," I said. "But you've stared at my naked body for far too long."

His gaze slipped down between my legs. "Yes, yes, you're right. But I enjoy watching you."

"Don't you have a vampire girlfriend somewhere around here?" I huffed, annoyed that he was too straightforward and not shy about staring.

He laughed out loud.

"No, I don't," he said. "I will grab you something to eat while you get dressed, okay?"

I was relieved to have some time to myself and collect my thoughts.

When he left, the haze of being in our own world disappeared, and I wondered if he had done something to me. Something to compel me to follow his instructions. My head felt clearer- and I was shocked at myself at what happened. His voice had a powerful magical energy behind it. Silky smooth, and compelling. Nothing like I've ever heard before, and I wanted to hear it again.

Chapter 7

Alana

Later that morning, James handed me a coconut shell. I took a sip from it and grimaced.

"Ew, I like my coconut juice chilled with lots of sugar," I complained at the warm, bitter drink, and he chuckled as we sat on the floor in his living room. He was carving out rocks with a knife after laying a handful of sea kelp and a coconut drink beside it. The sea kelp looked like it was burnt to a crisp after he fried it outdoors. It tasted so bitter, but I was starving.

I chewed on one end of the sea kelp, watching him work as he carved out weapons from a bunch of stones in front of him. He must be really bored here, I thought. There were no jobs, and the vampires lived day by day, surviving off of blood.

"I forgot that omegas have a sweet tooth," he said, the sound of metal carving against rock ringing in the hut.

"Have you been around many omegas?" I asked, wondering if he sucked the blood of any of them.

"A few. A very long time ago," he said with a faraway look in his eyes.

"Like as mates, or...food?"

His lips twitched, holding back a smile. "Food. But that's never going to happen again. I almost killed one with how greedy I became."

I was starting to realize why the vampires weren't welcome amongst my people.

He was dangerous.

"Did you do something to me earlier to wash like that in front of you?"

"I didn't," he said. "You wanted to do it, and I wanted to watch. That's all there was to it."

But I didn't believe him.

"We can't do that again," I protested, dropping the sea kelp on the clay plate. I didn't want to eat it anymore. Maybe I'd eat it in a few days when I was starving to death.

"And why not?"

"Your people are about to kill me, and you're not doing anything to prevent that," I said indignantly. He was acting like nothing had happened to me. That me living here was just super normal.

"Eat your food," he said instead, eying the abandoned cooked plant on my plate.

"No thanks," I said, shaking my head.

"What would you like to eat instead?" he asked, looking at me with full attention.

"It doesn't matter. I'm about to die soon," I said, crossing my arms and leaning against the wall. I looked down at the rope tied tight around my ankle. "Can you take the stupid rope off? It's not like I'll run around here. There are too many vampires around."

"If I take it off, will you tell me what you'd like to eat?"

"Sure," I said, unable to believe it when he dropped his tools and walked over to me. I stretched my foot out to him, and he grasped my foot in his hands. His cold fingers on my ankle sent tremors through my body. He deftly untied the complicated knot with his fingers, letting the rope drop to the floor. Was this a test or something? Or was he so sure of himself that I would run?

But later, I would plan my escape.

"So, what do you like to eat?" he asked, sitting in front of me. It still threw me off that he didn't have a scent. Even betas had a neutral similar scent to them. Alphas had strong masculine energies and scents about them. My scent of pineapple was prevalent since I hadn't taken a scent blocker in over twenty-four hours or a heat suppressant. I didn't know what I was more terrified of- to go into heat in the middle of nowhere or to have my blood sucked by vampires.

My body was still wet from the impromptu shower, but it was hot and muggy anyway, so it didn't matter.

"You don't have it here," I said.

"What's the food?" he insisted.

"Fine, burger and fries. And lots of fruits and maybe a salad," I said as my stomach growled. His eyebrows scrunched together at the mention of burger and fries.

"What's burger and fries?"

"Oh, you haven't lived in the city for years," I said. But he looked young, like in his twenties. I couldn't wrap my head around it that he was older than fifty-five. "It's just a slab of meat between two pieces of bread."

"You will have it then," he said, nodding. "Stay put, or you can get hurt by the others if you leave."

"Okay," I said, wondering how unlikely it would be for him to get a burger around here. When he left the hut, I got up and paced around the hut. I watched him through the makeshift door until he disappeared out of sight.

This was my only chance.

My heart started beating wildly as I looked back and forth between the outside world and the muggy hut.

I had to get out of here.

If I ran fast enough, maybe no one would catch me. When I thought I waited long enough, I opened the door an inch and looked out. James was nowhere around, and everywhere was empty since it was still daylight. Vampires weren't walking around right now.

I rubbed my palms nervously on my shorts as I took a step outside.

The sun was bright compared to the darkness in the windowless hut, so it took a moment for my eyes to adjust. I ensured no one was around before walking further away from the hut.

My heart was pounding like crazy as I tried to remember where we walked to get here. The cave entrance was somewhere around. I was scared vampires were staring at me from their homes as I ran in the general direction where I thought the secret cave was.

Sand flew around my face as I continued running south. I wasn't sure where in the world I was now. Everything was turning more eerie and more unfamiliar. The mud huts were bigger in this area, towering above me, and there were odd-looking massive cages with betas on the ground sitting with blank expressions. *Oh my god, I thought*. They probably let them out at night to feed the vampires.

I had to get the hell out of here before I was one of them.

Running in the opposite direction of where I'd seen the metal cage, I squinted my eyes, trying to figure out where to go next. The vampire dwelling was huge, and all I could see for miles were tall walls of rocks and stone, blocking me from the werewolf side. The only way was the entrance to the cave.

"Hey!" someone shouted from behind.

Fuck.

I started running faster, but it was useless. In a split second, I was grabbed and surrounded by three vampires. I knew what they were even before they grabbed me. I instantly regretted leaving the safety of the hut. Their cold bodies pressed against me on all sides, freezing me.

Their red eyes surrounded me- their bodies thin and hungry.

My throat tightened with fear when one pressed his lips to my throat. He had wild stringy brown hair matted with mud and dirt. His loincloth was filthy and littered with mud. They looked like young vampires who couldn't care less about the rules. But there were no rules when it came to their hunt.

"Omega blood," he breathed, his eyes rolling in the back of his head.

"Please, don't," I said, my voice trembling.

This could *not* be happening. My nightmare was actually happening, and there was nothing I could do to stop it. I started shaking. Then I felt his fangs graze my skin, and I screamed as I struggled against them.

"Release her," someone shouted, and I opened my eyes.

James stood in front of us like a vengeful angel. His eyes were glowing a brighter red, and his face set in a strict line. I breathed a sigh of relief when the vampires instantly let me go.

"Why can't we have her?" whined one of them.

"We need to wait for the full moon. Volgriff's orders," said James strictly as he held me by the arm. The grip from his fingers showed me that he wasn't happy with me running away. But I'd rather be stuck with him and his anger than get instantly murdered by vampires.

In the hut, James confronted me once we were alone again.

"What were you thinking, omega?!"

My back was pressed to the wall, and this raging vampire in front of me was unleashing his anger. I was getting angry, too, with every outburst. None of this made sense. I was the one who should be angry, not him.

"I wanted to escape," I said in a firm voice. I wasn't going to back down. "You're holding me here against my will. What did you expect?!"

He pressed both hands on the wall on either side of me, caging me in. He could be as dominating as he wanted to be, but I wasn't going to back down.

"This is for your own safety," he said slowly and evenly as if trying to make me understand like I was the unreasonable one. "You're the one who strolled into this camp all on your own, isn't that right?"

"Yes, but..."

"But nothing. Now it's my duty to make sure you stay alive," he said.

"You'll allow them to feed on me when it's the full moon?" I challenged.

"Yes."

"Then I want out!" I screamed, punching his chest, which felt like a brick wall. I pushed him, but he wasn't moving anywhere, keeping me trapped between his arms. He stood there silently, watching me. "I saw the betas. I saw what you do with them. You're all monsters."

I started shaking, and tears rolled down my eyes uncontrollably from my fear. I grew increasingly terrified of what was going to happen to me.

"Breathe," he said finally, encircling me with his arms. Pulling me against his bare chest. I couldn't control my panicked breaths and my tremors as I shook in his arms- remembering the near attack just now. Reminding me of my past. "Just breathe, Alana. I know. I know what you went through. I won't allow anything to happen to you, I promise with everything in my being. I promise you."

Rain pelted against the hut as he hugged me to him until my breathing slowed and I began calming down. My tremors stopped as I silently breathed him in, my tear-stained cheek pressed against his bare hard chest. Even though he didn't have a scent, he smelled like masculine sweat and hard work when I was close enough.

It was appealing and dark. A pull to my senses that I couldn't explain.

Chapter 8

Alana

While I laid on my makeshift bed of blankets on the hard ground, I listened to the rain pelting outside. James had gone out, and I didn't dare leave the hut this time. Maybe I'd try another escape attempt next time, but I was still shaken from earlier.

It was a close call.

I wondered if my family was looking for me and if they were worried about me at all. I began to regret isolating myself from them for so long. I missed my grandmother and wondered if she was faring well with my shop. The shop that I had taken care of like it was my baby.

The door burst open, letting in a shower of rain, and I sat straight up. James walked in through the door. I noticed his bloody hands as he smiled at me.

"Err, what did you do? Don't tell me you murdered an innocent beta," I said, staring at him in bewilderment.

"Come outside. I have a surprise for you," he said, holding the door open.

"But it's raining out," I whined. "I don't feel like getting wet."

His eyes flashed at my choice of words, and I blushed.

"Oh, don't you?" he said darkly. "Come, omega."

Rolling my eyes, I stood up and followed him outside- shielding my face from the harsh summer rain pouring outside. A severed leg of a sheep was sitting on the table at the front of the hut.

"Okay?" I said, staring wide-eyed.

"Your burger," he said proudly, slapping the shank. He took a rusty knife and began to shear off a small square of meat, then placed it over a small fire, sticking the meat on a makeshift skewer. I ran under the roof patch next to the fire to escape the rain. The small fire warmed my thighs while I stood next to him, watching him turn the meat around in circles.

It reminded me oddly of the time Lio and I roasted marshmallows. And the light fluttery feelings I had years ago.

I shook my head quickly to dispel the memories before they took me down the dark lane that I could never escape from once I was in it. The memories consumed me to the core, making me feel helpless and weak. I shuddered.

"Are you okay?" James asked, placing a hand on my arm.

"Yes," I said. "I was just remembering the time...sorry, never mind."

"Never apologize," he said in a hard voice, turning to me. His eyes locked onto mine, also remembering. A deep understanding between us. "I understand."

I nodded shakily, watching the piece of meat sizzle with tendrils of smoke floating above us. I was touched that he took the time to get me a real meal, even though it was rough. It spoke volumes of who he was at his core.

"I think it's done," I said. Then trying to lighten the situation.

"Where's the bread for the burger?"

"That was the only thing I couldn't obtain," he said, handing me the skewer. I blew on the meat.

"Then this will be barbeque, my next favorite meal," I said, smiling.

"I'll never get used to your type of food," he said, shaking his head.

"Want a bite?" I asked, bringing it to his mouth. His nose twitched, and his lips curled in disgust.

"I like my meat bloody," he declared. "That looks dry as fuck."

I giggled as I took a few bites of the meat. It was dry but not that bad, especially without any seasoning.

"Do you have salt?"

"Of course not. I don't have time to season my victims," he replied.

That very same night, a hole broke through the roof above me. It happened while I was trying to sleep, and a stream of water splashed across my face. I woke up sputtering. Sitting up, I quickly moved out of the way, looking up to see that there was a tiny hole where the rain was coming through.

Great.

"You okay?" asked James, groggily from the bed.

I quickly pulled the blanket from the ground, dragging it out of the way of the leak. The floor was slowly getting flooded.

"Do you have a bucket or something?" I asked.

"No," he said, opening one eye. "Come join me."

"Can't you just fix the leak?" I asked, desperate. The bed was way too small, and there was no way I was going to get on the bed with him.

"I'll work on it tomorrow," he said, turning onto his back. "I won't touch you, I promise. Just sleep."

My heart puttering in my chest, I gingerly walked over to the small bed and lay on the very edge of it. Even then, our bodies were only inches from each other. We were barely touching, but I could still feel the forbidden energy between us. I pulled the blanket over my head, watching the rain sprinkle into the hut and soaking the mud floor.

I lay there, listening to James breathing next to me. A few minutes passed, and I could tell he was still awake too. I was as still as a statue, trying not to make it awkward. I tried to breathe normally, but my scent was getting heavier in the air, overpowering every other smell in the hut. Deciding to get more comfortable, I turned onto my back and closed my eyes.

"Do you normally sleep at this time?" I whispered.

"Not really," he replied. "I'm usually out hunting."

"I don't want to change your routine or anything," I said. "You can still do what you do at night."

"I want to make sure you're safe," he said. "Do not worry about my comfort."

Somehow that touched me. A little part of my heart wondered if he was for real.

"How did I get myself into this situation?" I sighed.

"You were simply curious. Don't blame yourself."

"If only I had stayed at home and worked at my shop- none of this would have happened," I said.

"What kind of shop do you have?"

"I sell products for omegas," I said. It was my pride and joy. And I especially loved talking about it. "Stuff like candles, nesting products, and perfume."

"Sounds...interesting."

I looked over at him, seeing a thoughtful look on his face. "What is it?"

"Do you feel like you might go into heat? Considering you don't have any products for it here?"

"I mean, it could happen," I said. He suddenly reached over and touched my forehead with the back of his palm. His hand felt nice and cool to the touch. A warmth of fire simmered in my core and in between my legs. His touch ignited something foreign within me.

"You're warm," he said gruffly.

"Oh, it's nothing to worry about," I brushed off. "I'm always warm, and you're a vampire. Your temperature is a lot different from mine."

When he lifted his hand off my forehead, I reached out, grabbing his hand. His eyes widened in surprise, his red irises staring directly at me. I instantly released his hand, and he slowly turned towards me, lying on his side.

"What's going on, little omega?"

"I don't know what took over me. I'm sorry," I said, my face burning. I hope he couldn't see how embarrassed I was as I lay on my back. I felt his eyes boring into me as I lay there, contemplating whether to run out of his hut in embarrassment or just sleep on the flooded floor.

"Something tells me you're not too far from your heat," he said in a low voice.

Breathing hard, I turned away from him.

"I think...I'm just tired," I said, yawning loudly to cover the silence. After that, he stopped prying and asking me questions about myself.

Then I heard the sounds of his soft breathing when he finally fell asleep, mingling with the sound of the rain dripping.

Sometime in the middle of the night, I opened my eyes- restless. I was somehow lying in the center of the bed, right next to James, with our bodies touching and molded into each other. He was snoring heavily as I tried to move away from him. The movement of the bed startled him, and he grabbed my left thigh. My face burned as I lay there, not wanting to wake him. His hand was wide and powerful, holding me to him as he slept.

My pulse raced, and the wetness between my legs drenched my panties as I lay there. I tried to pry his hand off my thigh, but that only made him move up higher, going into intimate territory I wasn't prepared for.

His cool hand was heavy against my bare skin, and for some reason, it made my omega hormones go wild. My stomach clenched with desire, and the feeling in my breasts got heavier, begging to be touched and caressed by this vampire. *Was I attracted to him because he wasn't an alpha? Or because he was being protective of me?* I decided I needed to end this before things got out of control. I tried to shove his hand down, and suddenly his eyes snapped open in the dark.

He looked down at his hand clutching my thigh and immediately released me.

"Fuck, I'm sorry," he said groggily.

"Don't stop," I whispered, and he let out a low groan in the dark. I could see his cock standing straight out, uncovered by the cloth.

"Are you sure?"

"Yes," I said in a low voice, my gaze lowering. His dick was rock hard, and I couldn't help but stare. I waited for him to come to me, but he lay there on his side, his dick jutting out.

"Then I want you to come to me," he said. "If you want me, that is. I will not force you."

Swallowing out of nervousness, I turned to him and laid a hand on his chest- exploring him. He wasn't too hairy, and he wasn't hairless either. The planes of his muscles stood out, turning me on even more. My pussy tightened and clenched with arousal as I lifted my leg over his waist, and he rolled between my legs, settling above me.

"I want you," I said, my hand traveling downward until I grabbed ahold of his cock behind the loincloth.

He ripped his loincloth to the side, cock springing free.

Chapter 9

Alana

"Are you sure about this?" he grunted, his voice mixing with the rain pounding on the roof. I bit my lip nervously, watching him above me, intent on taking me. He was feeling the same way I was.

Horny as hell.

"Very," I said, quickly unbuttoning my shorts. I've never felt such a sexual urge in my life, and I wanted to quench it as soon as possible.

I needed to have him. I needed him deep inside of me.

"I'll help you," he said, his fingers digging into the waistband of my shorts and pulling them over my thighs. He dropped them on the edge of the bed and rubbed his hands over my bare thighs. His cool touch felt amazing against my warm skin. "Are you sure you're not in heat?"

"I'm sure," I said. "I would be in mortal pain, wouldn't I?"

"I can smell your pussy," he growled, and my breathing quickened as his hands gripped my thighs.

"Oh, that's so embarrassing," I said, blushing. I never had someone get that close to me.

"Let me taste your little pussy. Do you want that?"

"Oh god, yes," I said, breathing faster as he leaned down, pressing his cool lips against my upper thighs.

"You smell so good. Like pineapple."

I leaned back- absorbing the feeling of him kissing and sniffing my thighs all the way up my pussy. I ached for him to kiss me at my core.

Just a little bit higher.

The sounds of his kissing, mixed with the sounds of the dripping rain, made me comfortable in the dark with him. It was the hottest thing to ever happen in my life, and I wasn't going to stop it. I wanted him. And I wanted it bad.

With my pink panties still on, he outlined the shape of my pussy with his finger.

"Should I remove your pretty little panties?"

"Yes," I breathed.

"Do you want my middle finger deep inside your little pussy? Or my tongue?"

I knew my face was beet red by now. I had never been this bold and adventurous. This side of me had remained dormant for so many years.

"Your tongue, please."

"You have such good manners, little omega," he said gruffly, pulling my panties to the side. The chilly air wafted over my pussy. "Good little omegas deserve to be tongued down."

When the tip of his tongue touched my clit, I yelped at how cold his tongue was. It felt so incredible against my warm pussy.

"You're cold!"

"Should I stop?" he inquired, his breath cool against my pussy.

"No, please keep going," I begged, not wanting him to stop. The sensation was amazing. He proceeded to lick my pussy with the full wideness of his tongue. The chill made the sensations ten times stronger, my pussy clenching uncontrollably as he licked me in slow deep strokes. My slick folds opened under his tongue. When the brunt of his cold tongue hit my clit again, my legs automatically tried to close.

But his head was still between my legs, his tongue invading my pussy in deep strokes, blocking my legs from closing.

His tongue licked in circles around and around my throbbing clit. Slick seeped from my heated center down to my thighs as he licked and prodded. Then I felt myself stretching wide as he pressed his tongue inside.

"Mhm," he murmured, pumping his tongue deep inside my pussy.

"Ahh," I moaned as James sat up on his knees, pulling my thighs up, keeping his face pressed into my dripping wet center. Half my body was up in the air, my legs thrown over his shoulders as he feasted between my legs. "Oh, I can't hold it anymore!"

"Don't hold back," he said as he licked me repeatedly. Not allowing a drop of my slick to go to waste. "I love your pussy from this view. So open, delectable, and dripping for me."

I felt more liquid spurt from my pussy as I began to convulse. My thighs started shaking as he held my ass with both hands, holding me up to his face. His thumb slipped between my cheeks, rubbing against my anus. I screamed as I shook and trembled under his cold tongue.

"Oh, *moons*," I moaned when he finally lifted his face from my pussy. He smiled wickedly at me as I tried to catch my breath.

"How was it?"

"Amazing," I said as he gently set my legs back down on the bed.

My tense muscles were now relaxed. My pussy was still clenching and releasing slick as he lay next to me, covering his dick with the loincloth again. "What are you doing?"

"Next time," he said, smiling as I stared at him sleepily. "Get some rest now, little omega. We have a big day tomorrow."

"What are we doing tomorrow?" I asked, my eyes closing against my will. And before I knew it, I fell into a deep sleep, satisfied and secretly excited about the possibility of this vampire. *Could we be fated mates? Did he feel it too? Or was this a quick fuck to get it out of our system?*

If we were fated mates, then nature had taken a twisted turn for me.

The next morning, I groaned upon waking up. When I tried moving, I felt a pleasant ache between my legs, and the memories of last night rushed through my head.

Oh god.

I didn't feel James beside me in bed, but upon opening my eyes- I saw him sitting on a chair, watching me with a hooded expression.

"Erm, were you watching me sleep?" I asked.

"Good morning," he said, his eyes on me as he made his way to the bed. "I thought you'd never wake up."

I sat up, hugging the blanket to my chest and burning from embarrassment when I saw my underwear sitting on the bed right on top of the blanket. If I grabbed it too soon, he'd look at the underwear, so I held myself back. He sat very close to me, all hard and muscular, watching my face and my every move. I felt self-conscious like never before.

The memory of him eating me out last night with my thighs on his shoulders made my pussy tingle with desire.

"How did you sleep?" I asked, gulping as he wrapped his arm around my waist.

"I slept phenomenally," he replied. "I couldn't stop thinking about your delicious pussy. And how it tasted in my mouth last night."

I blushed, looking at my feet sticking out of the sheets.

"Well, it was all an accident," I said. A twinge of pain went through my stomach, and I pressed a hand to it. It passed after a few seconds. The pain wasn't something I'd felt before. I probably pulled a muscle or something last night when he was eating me out.

"What's wrong?"

"Nothing, it passed," I said, turning to him. He was looking at me, staring at my lips. Instinct made me lean towards him, and our lips met. The quiet of the hut made it even more romantic as our bodies meshed on the bed. My pussy clenched when I felt his cock pressing against my stomach. When the kiss ended, he was on top of me, and his eyes darkened with need.

"I don't think it was an accident," he growled, separating my legs with his knee. "You're dripping, little omega."

"Am I?" I asked hoarsely, wanting him more than ever. I needed him inside me, and the need for him scared me. "I want you, James. Please don't tease me."

"I want you too," he said, dipping his finger into my pussy. When he pulled his finger out, he held it up to the light, and I saw it shine with my clear slick. "Fuck, you're ready for me."

My face heated, seeing my slick all over his finger like that. Then he placed his finger against my mouth, and I opened my lips, aroused like nothing before.

"Oh, what are you doing?" I breathed.

"Taste," he said, jamming his finger in between my lips, forcing me to taste my scent as he crammed his finger into my mouth. This turned me on even more, as my pussy clenched hard. Then he removed his finger from my mouth when he was satisfied. "Good girl."

"Oh my," I replied when James settled his cock over me, brushing against my lower belly first so I could feel how thick he was.

"This thing is going inside you," he said. "Are you ready for me, sweetheart?"

"It's big," I gulped.

"Touch it first," he said gently, and I hesitantly reached out. My fingers wrapped around his thickness, feeling how hard he was. His dick felt smooth and cool to the touch. My pussy throbbed to have his cock inside me. *Oh, it would feel so good*. I guided him to my pussy, and he pushed his cock inside of me. This was so different than the night I was attacked on the beach.

"I thought it would hurt," I whispered as he slid his cock inside me.

"When both people want it..." he grunted as he watched my face for any hint of discomfort. "It shouldn't hurt. It should be fun and hot."

I closed my eyes as I felt his cock slide in and out of me. I wrapped my legs around his waist, pulling him deeper into me. I needed his cock to fill me up. My pussy clenched harder this time, and I nearly cried out. *Was this what real sex was like?* I wanted him more than ever, and I couldn't see reason at this moment. My belly ached to be filled to the hilt with his semen.

"Open your eyes," he commanded, and I opened them. "I want you to look at me while I make sweet love to you. Do you understand?"

"Yes," I breathed, unable to believe how hot this was. Every second of it made me want this all the time. "Fuck me harder. I'm ready."

"Okay, baby," he said, thrusting into my pussy. His cock stretched my pussy with every thrust. Faster and faster. Until his cold cock heated up, and we both exclaimed when he finally orgasmed. My breathing was accelerated, out of control as I tried to regain myself.

"Was that good?" I asked uncertainly, watching him take a few breaths. His face was unreadable and serious.

"That was the best sex I've ever had," he said, lowering his face to mine and kissing me hard. "Your pussy. My god."

"Is there something wrong with it?" I asked uncertainly.

"Absolutely not," he said harshly. "I've never had sex with an omega before. You have the best pussy in the world."

He rolled over, cuddling me to his chest. I touched his arms, feeling his muscles flex underneath as he showed off for me, and I smiled.

"And I've never had sex with a vampire," I said. "Actually, I've never been intimate with anyone after my…after what happened at the beach."

"Damn," he said slowly. "I guessed that by the way you stared at my dick. I thought there was something wrong with it, and it didn't meet your standards. Since obviously omegas need knots."

"No, of course not," I said, laughing. "You made sex less scary for me, and I want to thank you."

"Don't thank me," he replied. "I enjoyed myself just as much as you, don't get that wrong. Come, let's shower together. I have to make sure the damn barrel of water doesn't fall on you again."

"I'm just a little bit clumsy," I said as we made our way outside with my hand in his.

"Not just a little," he countered. "A lot."

"Hey!" I said, pulling my hand away from his, but he smiled and pulled me in for another kiss.

"You need a strong male to protect you, sweetheart," he said gruffly. His words sent twinges of butterflies in my belly again, turning me inside out. It would be nice to finally have someone at my side, taking care of me. But it was a fantasy that I couldn't indulge in. At anytime, I could get killed here.

James poured water over me as I scrubbed myself with soap. The water was warm from the sun, despite it raining like crazy last night. I have no idea what happened to me, but I was feeling all sorts of feelings when I was with him. We were naked under the sun as we took turns washing each other. My hands were bubbly from the soap as I rubbed his chest. He was hard and cool to the touch, like a marble statue. I felt a sudden twinge in my belly, and I bent over, gasping.

"I don't know what's happening to me," I said.

"Are you okay?" he asked, concern furrowing on his face, his hand on my lower back. I couldn't stand up straight as I doubled over in pain.

"What's going on with me?" I cried out at the sudden onset of pain. It came out of nowhere when he turned me on just by watching me.

"This isn't good," he said worriedly, splashing water on me to wash off the soap.

Shit. I was in heat.

"I think I'm..."

"In heat?" he asked, worry in his tone.

I tried to stand up straighter, but he quickly hurried over, wrapping a towel around me. He placed one hand on my back and one on my belly as he walked me back inside. He led me towards the only chair in the room, and I tried to sit, but I couldn't.

I was in too much pain. I collapsed on the bed instead, curled into fetal position as he sat beside me. My stomach and pussy were clenching tight with no relief.

"This is so painful," I groaned, holding myself as I waited for the tight feeling to pass. But it wasn't passing. And there was no relief except that of an alpha's knot. "I might die a slow, painful death."

"No, you won't," growled James. "I won't allow it."

My pussy clenched again, and slick began dripping from me, down my legs. I never imagined being this unprepared for my first heat.

This was an utter nightmare.

I needed the knot of an alpha to ease my pain through this heat. I would need not one but multiple alphas taking turns with me through my heat. And in this situation, I had none.

"I think I know what happened last night," I gasped out through my pain. "I had all the signs of my pre-heat. Which is why..."

"So none of it was real," said James, a tinge of disappointment in his voice. "But enough of that. I need to find a sex toy or some other for you..."

Just then, the door to the hut burst open, and I opened my bleary eyes to see the leader of the vampires, Volgriff.

"Looks like our little omega is in heat," he said, clapping his hands with a wild look in his eyes. He walked over to me in the bed. *What was he doing here? Was today the day I was going to die?*

"Get away from me," I said weakly, trying to roll away.

He gripped my shoulder and sniffed my neck. "You smell delicious during your heat. We will have such a grand feast. Do you agree,

James?"

"Looking forward to it," said James gruffly. "We should wait until her heat passes, though."

"No, no, this is the best time," said Volgriff. "We missed the full moon last night with the thunderstorm and all. So today, we will have a delicious feast. Bring her to my dwelling."

I looked over at James, who nodded quietly.

"What are you doing?" I asked, shocked as he lifted me in his arms. "James?"

Was I fucking delusional about him this whole time?

We were *not* fated mates, no matter what transpired between us. I tried punching him, but every move hurt me even more.

Outside, I realized I was attracting more attention to myself, so I instantly quieted when the other vampires watched us. We were going towards the biggest clay building in this hidden village. I cried out when my stomach tightened in pain again and slick drenched my thighs. I was still only wearing the towel, and I hugged it to my body for dear life.

"Shh Alana," said James.

"Please let me go," I begged. "I'll run as fast as I can. Just hold them off. I know you don't want to kill me."

Actually, I had no idea what his intentions were and if he wanted to kill me. I had no chance in hell against him. I was way smaller than him and I was in pain from my heat during the worst possible time.

"She smells divine," said Volgriff. "I've prepared a grand bed for her to keep her happy and comfy while we feast on her."

"Looks nice," said James.

I looked up, seeing a large white bed sitting outside the building.

The cage full of betas was sitting off to the side, in direct view of the bed. They looked withdrawn and tired as they watched us approach. And there were about fifteen vampires standing around the bed. I gulped with fear and worry.

They were waiting on their feast.

And I was on the menu tonight.

Chapter 10

Alana

My body was wracked in pain as James gently set me down on the soft bed. I briefly wondered how they got it here in the first place.

Did they do all this just for me? Just to kill me?

"James can have her first," ordered Volgriff. "He was the one who kept her nice and healthy for us until her heat. Go ahead, James, and have your fill. Then I will go next."

James nodded, climbing onto the bed and resting his hands on my knees.

"I want to help you, Alana," he whispered, an earnest look on his face. "It will help your pain."

I shook my head, tears silently going down my face. But I needed some kind of relief, even if it wasn't going to be a knot.

"In front of everyone?" I whispered. He was able to hear me above the racket with how laser-focused he was on me.

"We have to. Then I'll drink some of your blood in front of them too."

"Then, what?" I asked, scared of what he would say. And he didn't say anything to me, just watching me wordlessly, his hands still on my knees, waiting for me.

In spite of the pain, I spread my legs for him.

The towel hiked up to my stomach, my pussy exposed to everyone. I didn't dare look around to see what the vampires were doing, but from the sounds of it- it was nothing good.

Once my legs were spread for him, James pushed his loincloth to the side. This time, I was more than ready for him. My pussy clenched as I stared at his cock, hungry for him to enter me. For him to relieve some of the burning heat within me. We stared into each other's eyes as he plunged inside of me.

I cried out at the impact, and he covered my mouth with a kiss.

"It's just you and me," whispered James harshly against my lips as he plunged deeper inside me.

"I want more," I cried out, scratching his back as I tried pulling him deeper. He was relieving some of my pain, but it wasn't enough.

It wasn't enough for an omega in heat.

His hips pistoned into me, thrusting into me with all the force he could muster. I moaned at the impact. The jeers from the vampires around us made me nervous, but I focused on James and only him.

"I'm sorry, sweetheart," he said. "Your pussy is clenching a lot, needing a lot more than I could give. I'm so fucking sorry."

"Don't be sorry," I breathed against him as he pounded into me. "You're helping with the pain."

But I knew as soon as he pulled out of me, the pain would come back threefold, and I was terrified.

"I'm going to drink some of your blood now," he said. "Focus on my bite. Focus on the pleasure I'm about to give you."

He brought his lips to my neck, and I leaned my head to the left, closing my eyes so I didn't make eye contact with any of the hellions around us. He stopped thrusting momentarily, and then I felt the burn of his fangs puncture my skin. I cried out as he licked my skin, relieving the pain with his saliva.

My heated center clenched and released more slick as he started sucking on my blood. The coldness of his lips against my skin felt amazing, and I was getting so aroused to the point of climaxing just from him feeding on me.

He quickly pulled away, and I opened my eyes to see him licking his bloodstained lips.

"Why did you stop?" I asked.

"I don't want to lose control," he said gruffly, thrusting into me a couple more times. "Fuck, I'm going to come."

After a few more seconds, he pumped one last time into me despite me clinging onto his shoulders for dear life. When he pulled out, my pussy walls tightened again in furious pain. I started crying from the pain, and he looked panicked. He lifted me in his arms, carrying me off the bed.

"Where are you taking her?" demanded one of the vampires, punching him on the arm playfully.

"She's thirsty and needs a break," said James, breaking out of the circle of vampires.

"What's going on?" asked Volgriff, coming towards us. I noticed his hard-on right away, and I swallowed, remembering what he said about taking me next. My heart started beating faster. There was no way I would make it out of this alive. Either I'll die from my heat or at the hands of the vampires.

"She needs water," said James.

"Okay, I'll get some for her. No need to walk away," said Volgriff jogging towards the house.

I watched James's eyes flick back and forth. Then before I knew it, he began sprinting at top speed away from the vampires. As he ran, I wrapped my arms around him, clinging tightly for dear life. His comrades started running after us.

"I will get you to safety," breathed James under his breath as he continued running. I looked back, seeing that we were far ahead of the vampires.

James was fast, and he was determined.

My pain had come back in full force, crippling me again as I lay in his arms. It was horrible, and I couldn't concentrate on anything around me as I focused on the center of my pain. Right in my belly-clenching and releasing.

I opened my eyes to see that we were back in the complex cave that I had gone through.

"Where are the vampires?" I asked, through my pain.

"They're scared to come here," he muttered as he made his way to the other side. The opening to my side of the world. "Where can I take you for help? Even though I hate this, is there an alpha you trust?"

The pain spiraling through my belly caused me to cry out. I couldn't think straight. But there was only one alpha that I knew who could help me.

"The heat clinic. Take me there," I gasped as another sharp pain ripped through me.

Then all I saw was black.

James

She was unconscious in my arms.

Panic rolled through my body as I ran across the beach and to the roads. My feet were burning from the hot ground without shoes, and people stared at me like a spectacle as I zoomed past them. I knew I looked like a wild man compared to what they were used to. Everyone was fully clothed in her world, and I was careful not to make eye contact with anyone.

I ran past street vendors, stores and fruit stalls. I half-expected to see omega auctions, but I didn't see a single one. That must have been outlawed now. No one was close enough to see what I was as I sped past them, looking for anything that looked like a clinic. I never learned how to read, especially when vampires were discriminated against and not allowed to go to school with werewolf children.

I went down a back alleyway and saw a beta. He was smoking, sitting cross-legged on the ground.

"Do you know where the heat clinic is?" I asked him gruffly, with the omega still in my arms. His eyes widened when he looked at me, and I instantly wrapped my fingers around his throat. "Tell me, beta, before I suck all your blood dry and leave your corpse in the dumpster."

"It's over there," the beta choked out, dropping his cigarette. "It's the only heat clinic here. Everyone knows about it."

"Where?"

He pointed in the general direction of the clinic, his face red. "The blue building with the glass."

"Thank you," I said, looking at him in the eyes. I stared deep into his irises. "You will forget that you saw me. Nothing happened, and you will continue to smoke like the mindless idiot you are."

I released his throat, and he blinked, looking confused as he picked up his smoke again. I wish I could compel Alana to forget me but omegas and alphas were immune to compulsion. It was something about their genetic makeup. I ran in the direction the beta pointed out, looking for the blue building. When I finally saw it, I breathed a sigh of relief. The time was ticking, and Alana's condition was getting dire.

Standing in front of the building, a slew of nurses rushed out, seeing the omega in my arms.

"What's going on?" one asked without looking at me. She felt for Alana's pulse. "Bring the stretcher!"

"She's in heat," I said quickly, looking down in case they saw my eyes. But none of them were paying attention to me as I handed Alana over to them with a last kiss on her forehead.

Then I sprinted away from the clinic, my heart heavy. I hoped she would be okay. It was all my fault that she didn't get help before she went into heat. I couldn't betray my people earlier, but now I was considered a traitor because I followed my heart.

Chapter 11

Lio

"Quit spraying so much cologne," I told Owen, my team's beta.

I was zipping up the spandex suit that covered every inch of my body. Markus, the second alpha in my team, was already ready and impatiently waiting in his uniform, just like mine. There was a square opening covered by a cloth attached with velcro over our cocks. It was the only uniform that this heat clinic could think of that would make it easier for us to serve omegas in a professional manner.

"I want to smell good for the omegas," whined Owen, wiping his hand over his sleek black hair after setting down his cologne. "You know how much they love it."

"They love our knots better," growled Markus, the oldest of my pack, with gray streaks running through his short brown hair. He had a beard, while I preferred to stay clean-shaven. He knew exactly what the omegas liked, and he was a great asset to my team.

"We all work great together," I said, putting an end to it before Owen freaked out on Markus. "Ready to start our shift?"

Just then, a stern male voice over the intercom sounded :

"Ironfur pack to room 302. Ironfur Pack to room 302. We have a code yellow."

We all looked at each other.

This was an emergency. An omega near death.

"Let's fucking go!" I shouted at them, running out of our office and down the blinding white halls. We ran around stretchers and nurses, with my heart pounding wildly in my chest. I've never had an omega die, and it *wasn't* going to happen on my watch.

Owen burst through door 302, and we all piled in after him.

"Fuck," said Owen, quickly making his way over to the omega lying prone on the table with an oxygen mask over her face. Nurses were massaging her belly and trying to spread her cramped legs. "She's in bad shape, guys."

But when I stepped closer and saw her, my heart stopped.

It was Lana. *My* Alana that I grew up with. She had scars down her legs and a brutal bite mark on her neck. I wondered what had happened to her, especially when her grandmother and family called me, saying she was missing. *Did a pack of alphas ravage her?* But there was no time for questions now.

We needed to knot her and fast.

Owen had gone into emergency mode, tapping her face and lightly brushing a wet towel over her eyes. She needed to be awake for this, even for a brief moment. Protocol frowned on taking omegas who didn't actively give consent.

The nurses had successfully spread her legs, placing her feet into stirrups. Markus was already between her legs, sniffing her scent. Her scent wafted around the room, calling to us. I inhaled her scent in the air, sending my body into rut mode faster than I thought it would. I ripped off the velcro from my privates, and my cock sprang free. The sound awakened Alana, and she opened her eyes.

She looked disoriented at first as Owen pulled the oxygen mask off her face. Her pretty face was twisted in pain and flushed pink when she saw me. She tried to speak but could only croak out in pain.

"It hurts," she whispered, and I could hear her with my alpha hearing, even though there was loud beeping from the machines and nurses bustling around. "Lio, you're here."

"I got you, Lana," I growled, gripping my cock as I neared her. I tapped Markus on the shoulder to move from between her legs. "I'll knot her first. She knows me and trusts me."

"Please, Lio," she said, her voice tinged with desperation. "I feel like I'm dying."

"Do you consent to us knotting you?"

"Yes."

"Lio will take care of you," said Markus gruffly, moving aside for me. "I can feel her pain."

My breathing deepened, mingling with Alana's. Our bodies were ready to unite as one, for me to knot her fully until she was relieved. This wasn't an ordinary day. It was completely different with her. She had pushed me away for years, which was the only reason I became a professional knotter- thinking I would never have her. So many questions I wanted to ask her, but they could wait.

She needed me now.

I pumped my cock two times even though I was hard and ready to enter her. I stepped between her open legs as she looked away shyly. I pressed a finger into her dripping pussy, feeling her readiness. I could

81

tell she had been ready for more than a few hours. Her slick seeped down her bottom, waiting eagerly for her knot. She had the prettiest little pussy I'd ever seen. A small rosebud, waiting to be opened.

"Just relax now," Owen whispered in her ear, rubbing her arm.

"Here," said a nurse, handing me the stretchable condom. I quickly rolled it over my cock. It was sturdy and just came out a few years ago for alphas to use in this heat clinic. It was against the rule to impregnate an omega, or else we would lose our jobs.

Her pussy lips were bright with her heat, signaling that she was ready. My cock hung heavy and pulsing, with the end of it dripping in pre-cum, and my balls tightened.

Lining up my cock to her entrance, I pressed into her open pussy. I rubbed against her clit, our liquids mixing together. I would mark her with my scent for days, and I would smell like her this week. She was my project, my omega for how long her heat lasted. I would have no other omega while I tended to her.

I pushed into her, slow and steady, as not to shock her with the size. Even though her head was turned to the side, I saw her eyes widen in surprise at my invasion of her. I pushed in deeper, watching my cock disappear into her. The thin skin of her pussy stretched around my dick. The heat of her almost caused me to combust instantly. I closed my eyes and groaned with the bliss of being inside this elusive omega who came to *me* for help.

I pulled back and pushed back in, one inch at a time. Working my cock inside her. Her channel was tight, and her elasticity refused to budge. She had been in heat for too long. I pulled back again and pushed back in again, forcing her tightness to release. To let me in.

She was gasping for breath, and I knew this wasn't easy on her. This was the hardest part.

Markus stepped around me and went to stand on her other side. He started purring into her, his vibrations calming her. Her pussy began to relax around my thick cock, and I was able to push in deeper and massage her pussy walls with my cock.

"You're doing so good, baby," said Markus.

"She's taking Lio's cock like a good girl," said Owen, kissing her cheek. Her face flushed in embarrassment. She wasn't used to dirty talk, it looked like, but her pussy seemed to love it.

The way it opened up for me indicated she enjoyed this very much.

Her pussy swallowed my dick to the base, and we stayed like that for thirty seconds as I allowed her to adjust to my size. Her cunt trembled around me as I reached forward, massaging her belly. As soon as I felt her muscles start to relax and loosen, I began thrusting. I gripped the curve of her hips, her hourglass figure, as I pushed in and out of her. She keened loudly, and I knew she felt the tension loosening. Her pussy was accepting me at last as I dipped in and out of her.

Her full breasts were being cupped by Markus and Owen. The sight of them squeezing her breasts and her full nipples caused my balls to tighten even more. My hands caressed her thighs and met at her nub. Her round clitoris responded to my touch, and she shivered underneath me, moaning in reply.

Her cry awakened the alpha within me.

Her pitiful state caused me to feel overprotective of her. She was never going to go anywhere without me now. She should be getting fucked in a cozy nest filled with blankets, not in a cold, emotionless clinic.

"Alpha, you must knot her," said Owen, eying me as I thrust into her with slow, deliberate moves so she could get used to me. My hairy thighs slapped against her ass while her pussy walls squeezed around my cock.

"We're getting there," I grunted, grasping her by the hips as I rutted into her nice and hard until she cried out my name.

Her slick made squelching sounds the more I pounded into her. I slammed into her at a more frantic pace now. Her pussy stretched with every pump, squeezing me so hard that I groaned out loud. I gripped her ass cheeks and spread them, watching her little puckered hole clench and tighten with my thrusts. I crammed my cock into her as she screamed through her own orgasm, her pussy clenching and releasing around me.

She whimpered when I battered my cock at her cervix, deepening my penetration of her. Markus and Owen continued to whisper to her, massaging her breasts as I rammed into her one last time. I saw stars when I finally sprayed my cum inside the condom. I longed to directly spray inside her, but that would complicate things. My knot swelled bigger and bigger until it locked us in place.

"Good girl," said Markus. "Lio just wants to breed you. To make your belly round and full."

"What?!" she asked, panicked, trying to get up.

"No it's okay. I used a condom," I said quickly- upset that the thought of having my baby upset her. It was illogical of me, and I knew it wasn't realistic. Why would she want a baby with someone she had no interest in?

Alana sighed as the tension melted from her body.

"Finally, relief," she whimpered, dropping her head back against the white pillow on the hospital bed. Owen rubbed her hair and kissed her cheek, to which she smiled to.

"I'm glad you're feeling better now," I said, leaning against the edge of the bed and rubbing her belly to ease the knot inside of her. Her eyes fluttered in pleasure as I massaged her stomach.

"Your knot...it feels so good, Lio," she sighed, wiggling her ass. "It doesn't release me."

"Do you like that, little omega?" asked Markus gruffly, and her face reddened.

"A little bit," she confessed, and I grinned as I rubbed the bulge of my knot across her belly.

Chapter 12

Alana

"What happened to you, Alana?" asked Lio, touching the bite mark on my neck that a nurse was bandaging up. I felt sore all over my body. From my sleepless nights, stress, and being in heat. I couldn't tell him the truth of what happened to me. I couldn't risk James's life when he risked his life for mine.

"I don't remember," I said vaguely, not meeting his eyes. He tilted my head towards him gently with the tip of his finger. "I must have hit my head or something. When I opened my eyes, I was here"

Pity and sorrow swirled in behind his eyes.

I didn't feel good about lying, but I was conflicted. He continued rubbing my belly, massaging his knot into me. My legs were still spread wide on the stirrups as the handsome black-haired beta and the second older alpha looked at me. I felt exposed and vulnerable in this position.

"Hopefully, within the next few days, you'll remember what happened to you," said Lio, while gazing into my eyes. "And we will deal with the perpetrators. Only when you're ready."

But I wasn't attacked.

My heart longed to be with James again. The first person I ever purposely became intimate with. Every moment of being here without him pained me.

The beta placed a straw in my mouth, so I was grateful I didn't have to answer at that moment. The chilled water felt so good on my parched throat. I drank the water so fast that the beta had to pull the straw away for a moment.

"Slow down, sweetheart," he said gently, placing the straw against my tongue. "I'm Owen, your attendant. That's Markus, and the alpha knotted inside you right now is Lionel."

"I know, Lio," I said. I was too nervous to look down and see how he was knotted inside me. But every moment of it felt so good. I didn't want him to move, so when the knot started to go down- I was disappointed.

"This must be awkward, that you know each other," chuckled Owen, looking back and forth between us. He was probably wondering why Lio was working here when he knew an omega in his life.

But despite myself, I felt my face heating up again.

"Listen," said Lio, looking directly at me again. "I won't tell anyone. Not our family or friends that you were here. Unless you want me to."

"I would prefer no one knows," I said.

"Of course," he assured me quickly. "Even though this is nothing to be ashamed about, this is confidential."

Lio pulled out of me, and I scrunched my eyebrows together as the pain flared through my belly again. This time it was harsher and more demanding. Now that I felt a knot for the first time and that I had been stretched, the convulsions in my pussy were a lot worse.

"Markus, will knot you now," said Owen as he put away my cup of water.

I looked over at the second alpha named Markus. He had distinguished short brown hair with flecks of white and a neatly trimmed beard which I found attractive. I wondered why he was here when he could have found a nice omega.

Lio moved away to the side of the room to recover. Probably to get ready and knot me again. It felt weird being knotted by him when most of my life, I actively avoided him.

Markus quietly placed himself in front of me, lowering his head between my legs- sniffing me.

Did alphas like to smell their omegas before a rut?

His tight black spandex did not hide his growing cock as he ripped off the square of cloth hiding his cock. My eyes widened at the thickness of his penis under the lights. Large and purplish-looking, with his veins bulging, I noticed a curved metal piercing at the tip of it, and my mouth dropped open.

"Hi, I'm Markus," he said. His voice was heavy. Thick and full, like his cock.

"Hi, you're umm...," I said, unable to speak as I stared at his pierced member. He snapped a condom over it, rolling it up to the base like a doctor snapping gloves over his hands.

"Yes, it's pierced," he said, knowing what I was talking about. He must have gotten questioned about it by omegas before.

"Is it going to hurt?"

"Let's just say...it enhances the feeling," he grumbled with a serious expression. He was a big alpha, and I grew worried as he inhaled my scent even more. His cock was covered with the clear condom, dancing in front of me, waiting to take me. My pussy throbbed for him to enter me, sensing how near his penis was to my entrance.

Lio came around to my side and placed a finger over my clit, rubbing me until I started shaking with arousal.

"You're going to need me touching you," said Lio.

"Wait, what do you mean?" I asked.

At that moment, Markus plunged his cock inside me, and I yelped. His cock was thicker than anyone's I've ever felt, and the piercing rubbed against my pussy walls. It was a crazy new sensation between my legs that I never felt before. It stung but also aroused me even more. He was already inside me before I could lift my feet off the stirrups.

Owen was grasping my breasts from behind, his hands warm and comforting as he squeezed. Lio frantically rubbed my clit in circles.

"I'm rubbing your clit before he starts to pump into you," said Lio. "Many omegas are uncomfortable with his cock unless there's some kind of stimulation involved."

I enjoyed the sensation of Lio's finger rubbing my clit. My pussy clenched and pulsed around Markus.

"She's ready," said Markus, and my heart started beating faster. I braced myself for his pierced penis as his eyes darkened with arousal and domination. While Lio rubbed my clit, Markus slowly pulled back, and the piercing rubbed inside my pussy. I could feel it rubbing on the inside as I pressed my fist to my mouth. Every nerve ending in my pussy was sensitive, and feeling a foreign object inside me forced more slick to roll down my thighs.

"It feels so...different," I moaned as he pushed back inside me with a grunt.

"I want to put a baby in you," said Markus. "I'm breeding you today."

But he was wearing a condom.

"He likes to imagine," whispered Owen in my ear. His hot breath causing me to tremble. "He always wished to impregnate an omega."

Markus looked at me, seeing if I would be creeped out. But for some odd reason, it didn't.

"Yes, put a baby in me," I whispered, and Markus's eyebrows rose at me in surprise. It made me horny that Markus wanted to impregnate an omega so badly. And that I was the omega underneath him right now.

He thrust into me harder, making my legs bounce on the stirrups. His muscular thighs were covered in spandex and felt hot against me.

He pressed his palm against my belly as he pushed even deeper inside me.

"I will make you round with my baby, and then I will quit this job," he grunted. "To be with you forever."

"Yes, you're getting older," I gasped when his piercing pressed into my core. "Let's make a baby together, Markus."

Lio groaned upon listening to us, his lips covering my nipple and his fingers working faster around my clit. My breathing came out ragged as I neared my orgasm. The thick, pierced cock inside me was relentless, continuously pounding into me as I rose higher and higher.

"You're being such a good omega," Owen crooned. "Clench around his cock, baby."

Even though it was already tight in my pussy, I clenched around Markus's cock as hard as I could until Markus roared his pleasure. The condom filled with his hot semen as he pushed one last time into me. At the same time, I moaned my pleasure as waves of slick cascaded down my butt.

Markus's cock began swelling from the base, pushing deeper and pulsing inside me.

My pussy walls stretched until I screamed in pleasure as Lio rubbed me frantically. Markus's knot was like a thick cucumber deep inside me, swollen and locking us together.

"You're taking his knot so well," said Owen. "You look so hot glued to his knot."

"Oh," I moaned as Markus leaned over me and kissed me on the cheek. I opened my eyes in surprise and saw him staring into my face with trepidation. Like I would take offense at the kiss. Instead, I touched his face and rubbed his beard. "Thank you for your knot."

"My pleasure," he said, face glowing in pleasure. "I'll make sure my knot stays in you for as long as possible."

"How does his knot feel?" Lio asked me, popping his mouth from my breast.

"The piercing adds to it. It feels amazing," I said. "Thank you for knotting me too, Lio. I feel so much better."

"I might have to look into getting a piercing," said Lio with a thoughtful expression in his eyes.

"How many omegas do you usually help in a day?" I asked curiously.

"We're assigned two for a week, but since you were in critical condition- you will be our only omega," said Lio. Somehow, I liked the sound of those words coming from his lips. I don't think I could stand it if he was actively knotting a second omega in a room next to me.

"I would rather focus on this omega," said Markus gruffly. "It feels like a real pack, the family I always wanted."

"Markus, you need to focus on this clinic and get your head out of the clouds," muttered Owen.

"Shut it," said Markus.

It was big relief just laying there, with the brunt of the heat taken care of by these alphas, and I was grateful there was such a thing as a heat clinic. To get my needs taken care of quickly and then go about my business without having to be mated to any alpha. I never thought I would end up here. Not in a million years, but fate happened that I did.

"Your next treatment will be in the evening before you sleep for the night," said Owen.

"Okay," I said, looking down at the bulge on my stomach. For some reason, it turned me on to look, and my clit throbbed. My pussy had never been stretched like this before. I felt so full and content as Markus breathed hard above me, still coming down from his own high.

Chapter 13

Alana

"Good girl," said Owen, lightly rubbing my ass after the two alphas left the room. I had no idea how all of this worked and was grateful to have Owen be so supportive and kind even though I was a total stranger to him. I liked him, despite his naughty behavior during my knottings.

"Thank you," I said, blushing from his praise. "Do you think I can take a shower somewhere in this place?"

"Of course," said Owen. "We made this facility, especially for omegas and to cater to their every need during heats. We know it's not easy to keep tidy with all the bodily fluids everywhere, so we have a shower right here in the room."

"Oh good, so I don't have to walk far," I said, grateful as he helped me sit up with my hand on my stomach. My heat pangs were a dull ache now, but nothing like it was when I first arrived. He helped me off the bed, and I was self-conscious of my pure naked state. I had escaped the vampires with only a ripped-up thin towel around me, and I could see it discarded on the floor next to the bed. The bed was covered in liquid all over the plastic sheet from my knotting.

Embarrassed, I leaned into Owen for support as he walked me to the bathroom. The shower was spacious and surrounded by clear glass.

When I stepped into it, I fumbled with the shower knob. I heard Owen step into the shower, and I quickly turned to see that he had stripped down all his clothes. His chest had a smattering of hair which led down a thick dark line to his erect penis.

"What are you doing?" I asked in shock, trying not to stare at his member.

"It's my job to assist and wash you," he said, coming around to help me with the shower knobs. When he turned it on, it was the perfect temperature of warmth. It wasn't too hot to worsen my heat and fever, but it was warm enough to be comfortable. I closed my eyes, just standing there for a while. It felt amazing to finally stand under a real shower, not a makeshift one outside of a hut. A pang of sadness went through me at the memory. I sniffled, and I opened my eyes to see the beta soaping up a sponge. He began with my shoulders and my arms, pressing the sponge against my skin.

"This feels so good," I said, feeling weak as he lowered the sponge to my breasts, pressing all around.

"Good," he breathed, his eyes focused on my breasts. "Why are you crying, sweet omega?"

"I'm not," I sniffled.

"Something happened to you," he said gently, rubbing soap on my stomach now. "I'm sure it wasn't easy."

"If I told you what happened, you wouldn't believe me," I said.

"So you *do* remember what happened. Did you lie to your friend Lio?" He rubbed lower still, washing my legs next as I held onto the metal handle for balance.

"Maybe," I said vaguely, and he didn't question me further as he washed between my legs. I felt the sponge sliding back and forth on my pussy. He prodded my thighs open, and I spread for him while holding onto the handle.

"I will get your pussy nice and cleaned up for your alphas' knots," he muttered, grasping my hip with one hand while his other hand was between my legs, washing thoroughly. I felt the sponge slide between my folds, and my clit throbbed with the movement. My pussy clenched with desire at his attention. He swirled the sponge around my pussy, pressing harder on my clit area. I knew he was doing it on purpose as I felt his finger poking through the sponge to get to my clit. "You have quite a bit of hair there."

"I know. I didn't have a shaver for a while," I muttered.

"Don't worry, Markus loves his omegas hairy," said Owen, swirling soap over my pussy.

"How about Lio?" I asked curiously.

"I'm not too sure, actually," he said, pausing for a moment. "What would make you feel more comfortable?"

"Do you have a shaver? I want to shave real quick," I said, panic going through me. I never willingly had alphas look at me down there before, and I wasn't in tip-top shape. Lio had finally seen me naked, and he must have gotten disgusted by me. I still had feelings for him but never thought it would come to this point where he was treating me in his heat clinic.

"I'll do it for you," said Owen, producing a shaver out of nowhere with an impish gleam in his eyes.

"I mean, I can do it myself," I protested, but he was already kneeling between my legs.

"I want to do it. Taking care of omegas every need turns me on," the beta replied, already swiping the shaver up and down my pussy. "Spread your legs."

I spread my legs in the shower, and he shaved me vertically. He was speedy but meticulous, careful to get to every corner. I slowly relaxed, trusting him with shaving me. He knew what he was doing.

"Do you shave every omega who comes in?" I asked breathless with my arousal.

"Only if they want it," he said. "Anything you want, I'll give it to you. And all your base omega desires during heat will be taken care of by me." He rinsed off my pussy and rubbed the sponge over me again for good measure.

I was throbbing between my legs after his attentions, and I was horny as hell right now.

"That's crazy," I said. "So if I asked you to put a finger in my behind, you'd do it?"

"Yes, ma'am," he said gruffly. "Turn around."

"You're turning me on again. You're a naughty beta," I whimpered as he washed my ass next. He rubbed the sponge between my ass cheeks, rubbing up and down with a new squirt of soap.

"Sorry, baby," he said breathlessly. "I enjoy watching my omegas squirm under my hands. Bend down for me, please."

Feeling self-conscious, I bent down for him and spread my legs. I was aroused again, even though I orgasmed not too long ago. Being in heat wasn't something that could be relieved long term. My belly was already starting to clench, and my pussy dripped with hot slick again down my legs as he rubbed me between my ass cheeks. I swallowed, feeling hornier than ever, especially when he dropped the sponge and began washing me with his bare hands.

"Oh," I gasped when I felt his finger around my ass hole.

"I need to prepare you for when they take you at the same time," he said, rubbing my sphincter in circles. I clutched the metal handle, feeling my asshole start to respond to him, fluttering open and closed against his touches. Warmth of slick dripped from my anus the more he rubbed, and my breathing grew ragged.

"Are they going to do that today?" I asked.

"No, just on the last day of your heat to reward you," he said. "Instead of a lollipop, you'll get two cocks fucking you raw."

"Oh," I said, my face hot. "That sounds...delightful."

"It should be. Every minute of it," he said, poking his finger inside my ass. I gasped and jerked up with his finger stuck between my ass cheeks. "Relax, baby. I'm just training your little ass. Do you want Markus to take your ass when it happens?"

"Sorry, I never felt anything inside there before," I gasped, staring at the shower wall dripping with water and the smoke of the shower swirling around us. "I would prefer Lio to take my ass."

"Are you scared of the piercing?"

"Yes, sort of."

"Then maybe you should do something that you're scared of," he said, poking his finger deeper into my ass and thrusting into me now from behind. I bent down again to feel it go deeper, and my pussy gushed with slick. He pushed a second finger into my anus, and I yelped. "It just makes it more exciting, don't you think?"

"Yes," I said, unable to think straight. I wanted something in my pussy at the same time so badly. I wanted to be fucked in both places, and my heart beat with anticipation for my last heat day.

I couldn't imagine two thick cocks. One in my pussy and one in my ass.

"Would you like something in your pussy?" he asked, and I nodded eagerly. He placed his third finger into my pussy while two fingers were in my ass. I groaned in delight. Every sensation felt amazing. To be filled in both holes. "And you'll take my cock in your mouth all at the same time on your last day here."

"I've never had cock in my mouth," I said nervously. I've only read reviews of this heat clinic before out of curiosity one night while masturbating with my vibrator. Reading all the crazy reviews and what happened to omegas here turned me on like never before. Most omegas had left five stars, satisfied by the service here, and I was already impressed.

"Oh, you'll do amazing," said Owen, pressing up behind me while his fingers were inside me. His hard cock pressed between my ass cheeks. "You'll take my cock deep and nice without gagging. Can you do that?"

"I can try."

"Good girl," he said, removing his fingers from my pussy and ass. He turned the water off and wrapped me in a towel, helping me dry off as we stepped out of the shower. I was shivering with the pain from my heat. "I will give you a nice oil massage."

He led me out of the bathroom, and I saw that the nurses had changed out the plastic sheet on the bed for a clean one. The white floors had been mopped of all liquids, which would soon be dirtied again anyway.

"Where are all the other patients?" I asked.

"Every omega is treated in her own room in this clinic," said the beta, who started unwrapping the towel around me as I sat on the bed. "Lay on your back, please."

The plastic sheet made crinkly sounds underneath me as I lay on it with the towel under my back. I watched as Owen dried himself off and pulled on his scrubs. He wasn't wearing spandex like the alphas. Then he grabbed a yellow vial from a shelf, pouring it onto his hands as he approached me. My clit throbbed the closer he got, as I waited in anticipation for his warm hands to rub all over my body.

Chapter 14

Owen

The omega's pineapple scent was strong as she subtly watched me rub the oil between my hands. She was trying to be secretive about it, but I could tell how eager she was. All the signs were there.

Her chest heaved up and down as her breathing increased. The slight parting of her legs so I could see her swollen pussy lips and her toes curling in anticipation. My penis danced under my scrubs as I walked over to her side. I turned the vial over, watching the droplets of oil cover her perky full breasts. I enjoyed watching her breathe hard, with each droplet splashing against her beautiful caramel skin.

I started with her breasts.

I needed to feel the fullness of her breasts in my hands- to squeeze and massage until she came. I rubbed the oil around her right breast, using both hands to massage the oil into her skin.

Alana closed her eyes in bliss as I took over.

This was my favorite part of the job, even though I loved every aspect of it. But at the same time, I wished Lio could take on an omega, and we didn't have to deal with different omegas every week. I grew attached too easily, and it was hard to say goodbye after treatment. But sometimes, it wasn't hard to say bye to the bratty omegas who would usually have an attitude the moment they stepped into the clinic.

This omega was different, though. She was mysterious to me the moment she came into the clinic half-dead.

She was quiet and preferred not to talk- unlike most omegas I've seen.

I loved everything about her. The way her eyelashes fluttered in desire with each rub against her nipples and her breathing accelerating with my touch. I knew this was going to be a difficult parting, especially on my part.

"Do you like it when I oil your little nipples?" I asked her, watching her breathe sharply as I rolled her dark nipple with the pad of my thumb. Her nipple pebbled under my thumb, hard and aroused.

"Yes, it feels so good."

I rubbed the oil around her left breast, watching as she spread her legs a few more inches apart. Her breast was heavy in my palm as I cupped it, jiggling her breasts together. Oh, how I wanted to place my cock between her full breasts. To see how it felt to cum between her breasts and watch my cum dripping down her chin.

"You're spreading your legs for me," I observed the more I played with her breasts. She bit her lower lip at my observation, her face reddening. "What a good little omega you are, aren't you? Are you going to be our good omega during treatment?"

She smiled a little at my praise, her face glowing.

Good. I needed to help her forget whatever trauma she'd gone through before coming here.

"I'll try to," she breathed as I rubbed oil all over her stomach.

The curve of her hips and the dip of her belly button made my cock hard as fuck. I wanted to so badly fuck her, but it wouldn't be useful without a knot. I couldn't knot like an alpha. I rolled my fingers over both of her thighs next, pushing her legs farther apart the more I rubbed up and down. Her legs were drenched in oil, and she looked like a vision under the lights, her skin shining.

My fingers slipped between her inner thighs, and as I rolled up, her breath hitched in her throat as my fingers brushed her pussy folds. I rubbed higher still, spreading her legs even further apart until her pussy lips opened before me as I hovered over her body. Her pussy lips were covered in slick as I stared. Pink, bright, and juicy with her sticky clear slick. A drop of her wetness seeped to the plastic sheet as I spread her legs. I moved around the bed until I was standing in front of her, between her legs, her butt pushed up to the edge of the bed.

I wanted to lick her pussy clean, but she needed to be as moist as possible for her next treatment. I rubbed the top of her pussy in oil next and placed two fingers against her pussy folds, holding her open. I gazed at her pink nub, throbbing and pulsing as I unveiled it, pushing her hood aside. Using my other finger, I gently rubbed her little clit up and down. I watched her cheeks flush, and her thighs spread wider the more I teased her.

"Do you want me to make you feel good at this time? Or do you want to wait for your alphas?"

"Oh my god, please," she gasped out, her eyes fluttering open. "Please finish the job."

"Anything you want, sweetheart," I said. "Your clit is getting swollen the more I rub it. Does it need a little massage too?"

"Yes, please," she said.

I could hear the desperation in her voice.

Rubbing my finger harder against her exposed clit, I watched as her hips jerked up and her thighs shook.

She was close. I could feel it.

My finger was growing stickier with her wetness the more I rubbed her. I paused for a moment to grab a clean pink egg-shaped dildo with a long rubber handle that simulated a knot.

It wasn't the real thing, but it would do the job.

"Why did you stop?" she cried.

"I'm sorry, baby. I was just grabbing a little fun toy for you," I said, watching her chest flush with her heat. I pressed the pink egg into her tight hole, watching her pussy clamp around it the more I shoved it in her. "Does this feel good?"

"It does," she moaned.

I pushed the rubber egg inside her as I continued to rub her clit. The thin skin of her pussy stretched around the egg, suctioning it in deeper as I pulled the egg in and out each time. Then I pressed a button on the handle, and the egg began vibrating inside her little cunt. She yelled in surprise, feeling the sensation of the egg vibrating within her.

"Your little pussy is shaking and fluttering," I said, closely watching her glistening pussy lips clenching and releasing around the thick egg inside her. I shoved the toy even deeper inside her. She screamed when she shattered around it, her legs snapping wider one last time as she took it all in.

"Take it out!" she gasped, and I quickly pulled it out with a pop. The egg was dripping in her slick, and I smelled the toy.

Her pussy smelled amazing. Like pineapples, but muted down to a musky omega odor. It was mesmerizing. I closed my eyes, inhaling the smell of the toy as I brought it to my nose. Then I stuck my tongue out and licked the toy, tasting her saltiness on my tongue. She tasted even better than I thought she would.

"You taste scrumptious," I said, licking every drop of her wet release off the toy. I swirled the egg around her pussy to get some more of her sweetness as she lay there trying to catch her breath.

I licked off the egg again and put it in the sink. I washed my hands, and by the time I turned back, she had the sheets pulled up to her chest, and she was sitting up in bed with a pink glow to her cheeks.

"I'm hungry," she said, and I heard the sound of her stomach growl.

"You did so well," I said, touching her face with my pointer finger. "You deserve some good food because you were such a good little omega."

She blushed again, and I smiled. The nurse came in with a tray of food, and I watched my omega eating with gusto. She quickly ate the salmon like there was no tomorrow, wiping every piece of rice off the plate.

"This tastes so delicious," she said, digging into the oatmeal next. The nurse had said oatmeal was good for omegas losing a lot of liquids during their heats. I sat in the chair across from the bed, my dick getting harder the more she ate and shoveled down food through her plump lips. "Do I have any clothes to wear?"

"Most omegas dislike wearing clothes during their heats," I said. "But if you'd like, I can grab some lingerie for you if that will make you feel a little bit better."

"Yes, please," she said, smiling gratefully at me before downing a big glass of water.

Leaving her to finish her food, I walked out of the room, happy that the omega was finally feeling content and comfortable. She would be nice and full before her next treatment. She was already looking so much better than a few hours before.

As I walked towards the supply room in the building, I ran into Joey, another beta assistant.

"Dude, I heard about the code yellow. How is the omega?" asked Joey, his eyes wide with curiosity. He had floppy blond hair and brown eyes. A cheerful guy at most.

"She's doing much better," I said. "Took a little time for the alpha to knot her, but she's in way better shape after being successfully knotted."

"Awesome, my new omega is getting on my last nerves," said Joey. "She's refusing to get knotted by my team and requesting the biggest alpha Shigo who's out sick."

"Damn, I'm sorry," I said, grateful for Alana and her gentle but withdrawn spirit. I vowed to myself that we would make her happy and whole again before she left this clinic. "Listen, I need to find some lingerie for my omega. Good luck, man."

"Thanks, I need it."

Once in the supply room, I sifted through the rail of intimate lingerie for omegas. These were all brand new and had never been worn. I went through the size mediums which I believed was her size. I grabbed red lace panties and a matching lace bra. The panties were crotchless, and I imagined her pussy peeking between the hole. My dick hardened again.

Walking down the hall to Alana's room, I passed by Lio's office and overheard him arguing with Markus. Putting my ear to the door, I heard their hushed voices:

"The surveillance cameras showed a naked male, though," said Lio. "Why the fuck would he just dump her at the hospital without helping her?"

"He's probably a beta," said Markus and I flinched. I was tired of alphas referring to betas like we were nothing. Like we were trash of society. I knew Markus would never say that stuff in front of me.

"He had something to do with her," said Lio in a louder voice. "I want to show Lana the video and ask her if she remembers him. He doesn't look like anyone I know."

"I think you should hold off until tomorrow," said Markus.

I quickly walked to Alana's room, heart pounding. A male had dropped her off at the clinic. *Could it have been a past abusive boyfriend?*

There were so many questions simmering in my head.

Chapter 15

Lio

The footage I saw weighed heavy on my mind as I walked into Lana's room. Anger rose inside me at the thought of someone hurting her. Even though she didn't know it, she was special to me, and I was honored to help her, even though she never saw me as a potential mate.

"Just let it go," said Markus. "If you bring up the video with her, it'll ruin our rut. She needs us more than ever right now."

"You're right," I said as we neared her door. I adjusted the spandex I was wearing to make my growing dick more comfortable. "But the thought of someone hurting her..."

"It's terrible, but our job is to help her through her heat," said Markus. We had little involvement in an omega's personal life. But I knew Lana on a personal level. I knew her entire family, and we grew up together for fuck's sake.

In my heart and soul, I still wanted her. But she didn't feel the same way about me, and I needed to accept that.

I let out a long breath before opening the door. When I walked into the room and saw her pink pussy on display in her crotchless panties, my cock hardened instantly. All my worries and thoughts rushed out of the room. Her scent hung heavy in the air, intoxicating me to the fullest.

"Fuck," I whispered. She was ready and horny.

Owen was adjusting her bra for her, which had holes to display her nipples. She was smiling at something he said. Her large areolas were on display, with her nipples perfectly centered in the bra. My cock jumped, and I ripped off the covering at my dick. When Lana looked up and saw me, her cheeks reddened, and she tried closing her legs, but Owen had already strapped her legs up in the stirrups, thank fuck. If she closed her legs, I would have lost my mind. I needed her wide open.

"How are you feeling?" asked Markus gruffly, holding her hand and kissing it.

"Better, but the pain is coming back," she said, pulling his hand over her belly. He gently massaged her, and her cute face scrunched with pain. "I'm so glad you're here."

"I'm glad to be here too, baby," growled Markus. His eyes were laser-glued to her juicy breasts. I knew what he was thinking. He probably wanted to fuck her mindless until she was pregnant with his baby. He had expressed his feelings earlier, and he was infatuated with Lana more than any other omega who came in for treatment. Her innocence and nervousness about being knotted for the first time was every alpha's fantasy. "More than you know, sweet little omega."

"Markus, do you want to take her first?" I offered, watching their connection grow as they gazed into each other's eyes. It would be hot as fuck watching him knot into her again while she panicked from his piercing.

"I would love to," he said without breaking eye contact with her. I walked to her side and sat on a chair as I touched her right arm while Owen was on her other side.

Her skin was soft and warm under my hand as I pet her arm, moving to her shoulder and hair. I watched Markus settle in between her thighs, dipping his head between her legs. He inhaled deeply, smelling her pussy as much as possible. *Fuck, I should have gone first.* I couldn't wait until she was in the recovery room, where she would be in her nest so we could fuck her at the same time.

Markus

She smelled delicious. And I was ravenous for her.

I inhaled again, watching the omega's pussy dripping as I tasted her scent in the air, even without touching her yet. She smelled of fruits, particularly pineapple, which invigorated my older soul.

I craved her like air at this moment. All I saw was her eager pussy waiting for me.

"Fuck. You smell delicious," I said, unable to restrain myself any longer. "Do you taste as good as your scent?"

Alana blushed as I gazed at her.

"I...I don't know."

"I'll be the judge of that," I said, smashing my lips against her pussy, licking her ravenously. I licked in wild strokes until she moaned and rocked her hips on the bed, grinding in my face. Her liquid drops were precious on my tongue as I tasted her delicious sweetness. "Your taste is ingrained forever in my memory."

"May I have your knot?" she asked shyly, gazing down at me, lapping her up between her legs. "It really hurts Markus."

The sound of pain in her voice nearly broke me as I immediately released my cock to her service, the sound of the velcro resounding through the room. Owen began rolling her clit between his fingers, and Lio was kissing her neck while she blushed at his attentions, growing wetter for me.

This was the perfect time to plunge into her and breed her.

I groaned with annoyance as I yanked a condom out of the box and reluctantly rolled it up my dick. I hated using this fucking thing. I wanted to fuck her raw with nothing on at all. To pump her full of my seed and lock her in with my knot.

I rubbed the head of my dick between her pussy lips, admiring how her pussy made the condom shiny with her slick.

"Do you feel how big you made my dick?" I asked.

"Your little pussy made him big for you," said Owen, and her chest heaved with her fast breaths. Her legs trembled with desire as I watched her body respond to my cock pressing against her little hole.

"Should I keep pushing my dick inside of you, little omega?" I asked her, feeling her pussy clamp around me.

"Yes, please," she said, breathing hard and widening her legs for me. I pushed forward until I entered her. A couple of inches in, and she was already gasping. An older alpha's cock, like mine wasn't something she could easily get used to.

My balls hung heavy with my seed, and my cock felt like stone.

I pushed further into her as Owen strummed her clit like a toy to help her along. Her slick drenched her canal, making it easier to push further inside her. I watched as my cock entered her, enjoying the view of her pussy lips thinning around my cock.

"I want to fucking make you pregnant," I growled, and she blinked at the intensity of my words. I shoved the rest of my dick inside her hot little cunt, enjoying the way she opened and closed her mouth, silently watching me. Her eyes were glazed over with lust.

No other cock would please her. Not the way mine could.

I thrust savagely into her, my thigh muscles strong from my years here. Alana would get the best fucking in her life until she wished she was pregnant with my baby. Her pussy clenched and tightened on my dick the more I penetrated her. My cock felt so good in her warm little pussy in heat. She gripped the sides of the bed as I thrust into her. The squeezing and hot sensation on my cock was immaculate. My eyes rolled back as I felt my climax approaching fast. I wanted to fucking absorb this feeling for as long as possible.

"Oh, Markus," she moaned, biting her lip and moving her hips with mine. We were in sync now. We were in rhythm as I fucked her on the hospital bed.

She would get the best service possible from one of the most coveted alphas in this clinic.

I vowed to give her every inch of my cock and possibly my soul.

I pushed in and out, our liquids making squelching sounds throughout the room. Lio was stroking his cock as he gazed at our intense mating session. Owen was licking his lips as he watched my cock pound into her pink slit while he rubbed her engorged clitoris.

"I'm going to cum deep inside you," I growled, feeling my cock turn hotter and warmer as her pussy walls squeezed around me.

Owen rubbed her clit harder and faster to make her cum at the same time as myself. Her hands gripped the sheets tighter as she yelled, orgasming around my cock.

Then I came.

I didn't hold back as my dick gushed into the condom deep inside her cunt. I gripped her hands in mine as I released powerfully into her. I gasped through my breaths, watching her as she opened her eyes, also gasping. My cock swelled, pulling her pussy closer to me as we locked together.

Leaning down to her, I brought my face to hers. My heart was pounding hard.

"May I?" I asked, and she nodded.

It was against the rules, but I kissed her directly on the lips anyways. Her lips were soft and pliant under mine. My first kiss sent me to the skies at that very moment. I wanted to relive this moment over and over.

"Markus," Lio barked, and I quickly broke the kiss.

Her eyes were downcast as she felt rejected at that moment.

"It's against the rules to kiss omegas," I said to her. She needed to know. "They don't want omegas to get attached to the care team."

"Then why did you kiss me?" she asked softly, looking back up at me as I clutched her hands. My heart beat faster when she looked at me like that. Her small hands trembled beneath mine, and a wave of protective instinct came over me.

"The urge came over me," I said truthfully. "That was my first kiss in twelve years. I've never felt like this with any other omega."

"Mark, that's enough, man," warned Lio. Then to Alana. "Don't think too much about it. We're professionals and hope to keep it that way."

"Of course," she said, nodding. She looked more hurt than ever, laying there in that bed while knotted to me. I brought my hands to the sides of her face and looked her in the eyes.

"Don't be sad, Alana," I said, my heart nearly bursting in guilt. "Maybe the condom will break, and you'll be impregnated with my baby. Then we'll run away together from this place."

She giggled, and I was thankful to make her laugh. She needed to stay happy and content during her time with us. We were the best knotting team in the entire clinic, and I shouldn't have kissed her.

But I didn't regret it one bit.

Chapter 16

Alana

The next morning, a nurse handed me a bunch of forms when I woke up, and she was explaining each of them as she watched me sign the papers with her hawk-eyed expression.

"This one is for accidental pregnancy," she explained, slapping another sheet of paper on top of the one I had already signed. "Your care team is not liable for any pregnancies if that should happen. We have a ninety-nine percent chance that will not happen, but if it does and the alphas want to be part of the baby's life, you will agree to be their omega if they so choose."

So there was a one percent chance of getting pregnant....

"Cool," I said, signing the form with my drawn-out cursive that made the nurse impatient, but she kept on a fake smile plastered to her face. "What's the next one?"

"This one is a mating mark disclaimer, in case an alpha marks you accidentally," she said, her red fingernails pressing on top of the page. "Any questions?"

"Well, what happens if they mark me?" I asked.

"Then you're supposed to be their omega until death do you part," she said like I asked the craziest question ever.

Gulp. I had no idea mating marks were *that* serious. Maybe being here was a horrible idea, but I could already feel the pain brewing in my belly, ready for the painful squeezing that would happen in a few minutes.

"It never happened before," said Owen, comfortingly squeezing my elbow.

"Oh, okay," I said, signing the form. My alpha team didn't look that stupid to mark me. *But what about Markus's kiss?* He was unpredictable, and my heart pounded faster at the thought of him.

"Alright, that is all," said the nurse, gathering up the papers onto her clipboard. "Rest up until your next treatment. Owen will make sure you're ready for Lio and Markus before they arrive. Have a good day."

"Thanks, you too," I said, feeling embarrassed that all I'd be doing was lying on my back and taking in huge cocks. But the nurses around here seemed used to it like it was a normal everyday occurrence.

When the nurse left, Owen closed the door behind her and walked back to me, clearing all my breakfast stuff to the side for the cleaning crew.

"How is the heat feeling?" he asked me as I stretched and yawned on the bed. I pulled off the sheets, still in my sexy but dirty lingerie.

"More manageable," I said. "At least I can move around a little, but my pussy is sore as hell. Markus's cock is something else."

Owen chuckled and helped me off the bed.

"That's a common complaint if you take on Markus," he said. "The soreness should improve in a couple of days or when aroused. You'll keep craving it until your heat is over."

"I had dreams of being knotted over and over," I admitted, my face heating as he helped walk me to the bathroom to get cleaned up. I also dreamt about James but needed to forget about my encounter with the vampires and focus on getting through my heat.

"That means we're doing our job right," he said, smiling, and my pussy throbbed with excitement for what the day would hold.

Over the next few days, I was stretched and knotted in all kinds of ways that I could think of. I had grown more attached to Lio than I could ever admit. Markus and Owen had snuck into my heart, surprisingly, even when I swore off an alpha pack forever.

It was my last day there, and I was lying in my nest in the recovery room while Owen was getting me ready. The cushions under me were soft and plush compared to the rock-hard hospital bed. I was wearing black lingerie today, with black lipstick and my hair wild around my face. I wanted to look sexy and cute on my last day of treatment.

"You'll be getting double fucked today," said Owen, adjusting my legs on the cushion so I was spread out for the alphas before they arrived. The alphas had instructed Owen to keep me always spread upon entering. "Spread your pussy lips for me. Lio will be arriving any second now."

My heart beat fast as I dipped my hand between my legs. Using my fingers, I spread my pussy lips feeling the air hit my wet hole.

"Is that good?" I asked, getting hornier as Owen gazed at me.

"Yes, what a good omega you are," he said, adjusting my fingers to open up my pussy more. "You're going to make your alphas so happy when they see you all cuddly in your nest with your legs open and pussy ready for them. Lio will get so hard just for you, and Markus will put a baby in you. Just like you want."

"Thank you," I said breathlessly, enjoying his play. Owen went to my side, slipping his hands underneath me and gripping my ass cheeks. Then he spread my ass cheeks wide until I could feel my anus clenching against being spread like that.

When the door to the recovery room opened, I felt my pussy dripping as Lio and Markus gazed at me. Owen shifted to let them have a clearer view of my pussy and ass hole spread out for them.

It was like magnet when they walked to me.

With every step, my pulse accelerated, and my scent thickened. My pussy clenched with anticipation as I struggled to keep my pussy lips open and not let it slip from my fingers with all the slick I was producing.

"She's ready and open just like you requested," said Owen.

Markus and Lio both ripped off the velcro at the same time. The sound of the fabric echoed through the cozy nesting room. My pussy dripped even more at the sound. I was pretty much trained to get horny when I heard it now. Maybe they did it on purpose to omegas.

"Fuck," said Lio, kneeling between my legs. He ran a finger across my bald pussy, and his lips turned up in a smile. "You're nicely shaved today, Lana."

I almost convulsed when he called me by that pet name. The name he called me throughout my entire life.

Markus began touching my ass hole, tickling around my anus. Lio's finger dipped into my pussy, swirling my slick around.

"Give me some of that slick," said Markus, and Lio stuck his finger deep into my pussy until I clenched. Slick dripped down my ass cheeks, and Markus grumbled in delight, coating some liquid around my anus with his little finger.

"There you go," said Lio. "Markus will take your ass, and I will take your pussy. But first, we need to play with both holes. Is that okay with you, Lana?"

When he looked at me like that, with desire brewing in his handsome face, my heart pit pattered wildly in my chest. The hottest professional knotter on the island was all mine.

"I'm scared," I whispered.

"Of?"

"I never took dick...in my...behind," I explained, still shy to talk so crassly even though I was spread wide open for them. "Especially a pierced one. Would it be safe?"

"We've done it several times before," said Lio with a twinkle in his eyes. "You'll be fine. If it's too painful, we'll use a safe word."

"What's the safe word?"

"Pineapple."

"Okay," I said, repeating the word repeatedly in my head so I didn't forget. *Pineapple. Pineapple.*

Markus and Lio's fingers were moving around my pussy and my ass, exploring all my hidden crevices. Lio pinched my clit lightly, and I cried out. Every touch zinged through my body, almost always toppling me into an orgasm.

I closed my eyes, feeling all the sensations on my body.

Owen pulled my nipple into his mouth, and I groaned with ecstasy when Markus pushed his finger into my ass at the same time. Lio already had two fingers inside my pussy, thrusting and exploring.

"Juicy little pussy," said Lio. "I think we gave proper treatment to her pussy. Isn't that right, Markus?"

"We did," said Markus, who was intently focusing on my anus. "You just need to stretch that pussy out one last time today."

Their dirty talk was enough to get me off as my holes clenched tight around their fingers. I was so aroused I couldn't focus or think straight while they played endlessly with my privates before they would double-knot me.

"Lana, are you ready for me to stretch out your pussy one last time?" asked Lio.

"I'm ready," I squeaked. I wasn't prepared for all this stimulation during our first group treatment. I was terrified of Markus's cock going inside my ass, but I whispered the safe word to myself to remember. My curiosity got the better of me because all they did was make me feel good for days.

Lio stretched out on the floor, pulling me on top of him.

"Lay on me, and Markus will have easy access to your ass," said Lio. He smelled of fresh cologne as I leaned over him. While I did that, I thirstily aligned my pussy with his hard cock, and it slid in. "You already know what to do, bad little omega."

I felt a slap on my rear from Markus, and I yelped.

"Was she being bad?" asked Markus.

"It's okay," grunted Lio as I laid my chin against his shoulder while Markus spread my ass cheeks apart. Lio held onto my waist as I felt the tip of Markus's cock spear into my anus. I cried out at the initial burn.

His dick was a lot bigger than his fingers. But I wasn't ready to yell out the safe word.

I wanted to be fucked in both holes so badly. Owen stood over me, pulling down his scrub pants. His cock stood straight out, ready for my mouth.

"Are you ready for my cock in your pretty mouth?" asked Owen, hovering over my head. His cock was directly above me, with his hairy balls underneath. His musky smell of hard work and sex made my pussy clench.

"Yes, please," I said.

"Open your mouth wide, baby," said Owen, and I obeyed.

I opened my mouth, trying to take him in all the way. His cock was shorter than the alphas, but it was thick as I swirled my tongue around the tip. Owen leaned against the wall, groaning, his hairy thighs on either side of my face.

At the same time, Markus pushed further into me, increasing the burning feeling from my behind, but his piercing stimulated all my nerve endings. I felt like I might finally slick from my anus today. Lio was impatiently moving his hips under me for some friction, his cock pumping in and out of my pussy.

"I'm going to slide into your ass now," warned Markus. "I can stop at any time, even though it will be mighty hard."

Chapter 17

Alana

"Okay," I said, my voice muffled by the cock in my mouth. My body stiffened. Waiting for the impact into my ass.

"Relax, Alana," said Markus. "Just relax and let your muscles loose. Pretend nothing is happening to your ass right now."

But something huge was about to enter me...

At that moment, he pushed his cock deeper inside my ass, and I gasped. I moaned when he pushed it in deeper. Three heavy cocks were inside me now. One in my mouth, one in my pussy, and one in my ass. It was a symphony of pulls, grunts, and thrusting into my holes for the next few minutes. I nearly gagged a few times when Owen pushed too deep, and I soon forgot it when Lio's cock hit my G-spot, sending me into oblivion.

Pushing and pulling. Thrusting and groaning.

I bobbed my head as I sucked and slurped. Owen groaned with pleasure, and Markus slapped my ass like a horse's rump.

"So good," groaned Lio, watching me suck off Owen's dick. I swirled my tongue around the crown of his penis. The two alphas had taken over, lifting me up and down. Forward and backward to please their cocks.

My body was tugged in all different directions. It felt different and amazing to be used in this way. I never thought an omega would have fun doing this, but it was something I had missed out on for so long.

Owen exploded in my mouth, pushing deeper into my mouth as I swallowed. My pussy was dripping as I licked and swallowed every drop from his length. I wanted to taste it for once in my life. To experience all the sexy and dirty things that happened with it because I wasn't sure when it would happen again.

Owen grasped my hair, rubbing my head back and forth as I licked and swallowed.

"What a good little omega. You enjoy sucking cock, huh?" Owen crooned, his thighs trembling from his powerful orgasm that I caused. I proudly licked off the tip of his cock, and he collapsed on the cushions surrounding my nest.

I turned back to Lio and focused on the ride these two alphas were giving me. My pussy was stretched tight around Lio's cock as I rode him with his strong hands guiding my hips.

Wetness seeped down my pussy and my anus, keeping both cocks plenty lubricated. I clenched both holes to help them along.

"Fuck," said Markus from behind, placing his lips on my shoulder.

"Don't bite me," I yelped. The nurse's disclaimer forms flashed across my vision.

"I want to mark you so bad. I'm at the edge now," said Markus, his teeth grazing my skin as he climaxed. I shut my eyes tight, hoping he wouldn't mark me, and he didn't. Lio was staring into my face when he ejaculated at the same time. I looked back into his eyes, knowing we wouldn't have this connection again.

"Lana...I," started Lio, and I held my breath, worried about what he'd say next.

"Yes?"

Both their cocks started swelling, and my breathing accelerated.

I was nervous being stretched even farther. But they rolled me between them in my cozy nest of blankets to get into a more comfortable position.

"I was going to say that I have feelings for you, Lana," said Lio. "I know I've said it before."

I didn't know what to think. Markus rubbed my back, his large hand splayed across my skin, warming me. My heat was over, and this last knotting ensured I wouldn't be in pain at all. I only felt a few twinges this morning but nothing serious.

"Lio, I don't know," I said, trying to catch my breath. I felt their warm bodies press me in between while my pussy and ass were full of cock. "I'm not ready for a relationship yet. I'm sorry, Lio."

"I understand," he whispered, brushing a strand of hair from my eyes. "It was against protocol for me to even say that. I'm the one who should be sorry. You came in as a vulnerable omega in heat, and I shouldn't take advantage of the after-knotting glow."

I smiled at his choice of words, reveling at the touch of his palm on my cheek. It all just felt so comfortable and warm. Then I closed my eyes, just to feel this moment forever. To know what having a pack felt like.

I didn't realize I had fallen asleep until Lio tapped me awake. Both Markus and Lio's knots had deflated, releasing my body. Owen was nowhere to be found in the room.

"Oh, sorry," I said, stretching between them. I was sore all over, but it was a good kind of sore.

I would remember this day for the rest of my life.

And I would remember James risking his life for me. I hadn't had time to process it all during my stay here at the clinic, but I would write everything down in my diary to never forget what happened and how I ended up at the heat clinic for the first time in my life.

"I have something for you to look at," said Lio, pulling his phone out.

"Sure," I said.

"Lio, it's not important," said Markus but Lio didn't listen as he pulled up a video. I rolled onto my stomach to see. He pressed play on the grainy video. It was surveillance footage of the clinic's grounds.

My heart stopped when I saw a familiar figure. A pale figure with no clothes holding me limp in his arms as he dropped me off at the clinic's entrance. My eyes widened, and my heart pained to see James run away with no hope in his life. Unable to live with his people or mine.

"You're getting emotional," observed Lio, dabbing a tissue on my face as tears rolled down.

I didn't think seeing James on camera like that would affect me. He had affected me more than anyone I ever met, and he had real true feelings for me that couldn't be faked.

"No, I'm not," I said quickly, looking away. "It's just horrible to see myself in that way. Frail and weak. It was the most horrible day of my life."

"So, do you remember what happened to you?"

"No," I said, realizing my mistake. "It just looks terrible."

"Don't lie to me, Lana," he said in a softer voice.

I swallowed, still looking away from him so he couldn't see how hard this was for me.

"I'm not comfortable sharing right now," I said.

"Alright," he said with shortness in his tone. He sat up, stuffing his phone in the pocket of his spandex. "I'm sorry I brought it up as a friend and as someone who cares about you. Clearly, you don't care."

"I do care," I protested, but he stood up and walked to the door. *Why was he acting like this?* I didn't expect him to get so upset just because I wasn't telling him everything.

"I'll let the nurse know that you can be discharged now. It's been a fantastic visit, and we hope you use our services again," said Lio.

With that, he slammed the door, and my eyes widened in shock.

"What?" I said.

"He has strong feelings for you," said Markus gently, also getting up. "I want to apologize on behalf of his rude actions. He normally never behaves like that, but you affect him, little omega."

"Do I affect you too?" I asked.

"You do," he said, nodding with a sad curve to his plump lips. "It was a pleasure helping you through your heat. I wish I had met you under different circumstances."

"I know," I said, and just then Owen walked in.

"You can't leave without saying goodbye to me," he declared, strolling over to me with a new gleam in his eye after the blowjob I gave him. He sat down next to me, pulling me in for a hug, and Markus

125

joined in, too hugging me from behind.

"I'll miss you guys," I said when they finally released me. "Say bye to Lio for me. When he calms down, tell him no hard feelings from me."

"We will," said Owen.

Later after I was washed and dressed, I soon regretted my words about no hard feelings when I saw my twin brother, Adam, waiting in his car outside the heat clinic. *Did Lio tell my family I was here? Did he take it that far because he was angry?*

I was fuming when I walked to the car.

I was finally wearing normal clothes, which felt heavy on my skin with every step to the car. It felt weird after being naked for so many days.

I opened the door to the passenger side and sat inside.

"Hey, sister," said Adam, studying my face. "You okay?"

"Yes, I am," I gritted out through my teeth. "Did Lio tell you I was here?"

"He didn't want to, but I was worried about you," said Adam, not driving yet, but his hands were on the steering wheel. "The whole family's worried about you, Alana. But when I called Lio, he hesitated when I asked if you were here. I even threatened that I would break into the heat clinic if he didn't tell me."

I let out a long breath, embarrassed and afraid of what Adam was thinking about me.

"Does anyone else know?"

"No, just me. But the family knows I'm bringing you home now," said Adam. "Listen, I won't ask any questions about how you got here. I don't care to know, and I won't tell anyone. I'm just glad you're safe."

I sighed.

"Thank you, Adam."

We were close growing up despite the fact I moved out, and he was the best secret keeper in the world. It touched my heart that he had driven here to get me instead of creating video games which he loved to do in our parents' basement. Even though we had gotten older and grew further apart, he still cared, and that meant the world to me.

"Man, this clinic is fucking far," said Adam, honking his horn at a bunch of cars on the road. He flipped a finger out the window at someone, and I cringed in my seat. He still hadn't worked on his road rage issues. "I need to get back home. I think I may have a break-through."

"Oh, a new game?"

"Yeah, I need to develop it some more before I launch it tomorrow," he said. Our fathers didn't approve of what he was doing and they begged him to play sports or find a real job instead, but he had his own mind. I was the calmer, more logical twin and usually reigned him in when things went too far.

When we finally arrived at my family's home, I saw everyone outside. My mother, Tiana, and all my fathers. Grandma Bianca and my two younger sisters, Roxanne and Sarah all waiting eagerly for me.

"Shit, Mom is crying," I said while he parked the car in the huge driveway. "I don't know what to tell them."

"Say you got stranded somewhere," said Adam. "And also...you might want to cover that bite mark on your neck."

"Shit," I said again, looking into the mirror above me. The two puncture marks from James were turning purple and bruised. I tried pulling up my shirt to cover it but to no avail.

I would have to make up a fake story about it.

Chapter 18

Alana

After the family gathering and lots of hugs with bogus explanations on my part of where I'd been- I was glad to be finally sitting in Grandma's house in my favorite spot. It was tough fending off my family's questions, but I had told them that I was stranded in a cave system on the beach, which was partially true. My mother had cooked a gourmet meal with the help of my sisters, so I spent the entire day there catching up with everyone while Adam hid out in the basement with his computers.

But now I leaned back in Grandpa's old armchair, drinking hot chocolate and absorbing the smell of the apple pie that Grandma was making in the kitchen. As I sat in the armchair, I watched the sunset from the living room, sitting in wonderful silence.

Alone at last.

Everything that happened to me in the last couple of weeks felt like it was all a dream. I took a sip of the hot chocolate, the sweetness of it settling on my tongue. I couldn't believe I was back home again. I would check on my beloved shop tomorrow. Setting my drink down on the coffee table in front of me, I opened my diary on my lap and began writing:

08/03/14

Dear diary,

I finally found the guy I was looking for. He was a vampire, out of all freaking creatures. Do I still think about him? Yes, I do. He has a hold on my heart that I can't escape. A hold that no one else would understand. He understood the darkest parts of my soul. He was there the night I was attacked. The night we slept together in his tiny bed with the rain dripping into his hut was magical. The way he gently touched me when he realized I was scared of him. And I will never forget the way he caught the shower bucket from falling on me. My heart just beats faster thinking about it.

Lio...where do I start with him? How do I sort out my complicated feelings for him?

If I had never met the vampire- Lio would undoubtedly be my forever mate. Him, Markus and Owen, my forever pack. I would be content. But is that enough? Without James?

"Alana," said Grandma, breaking me out of my writing trance.

"Mhm?" I asked, still trying to write, but gave up, closing the book.

"Here's a little treat to go with your hot chocolate," sang Grandma, handing me a plate with a scrumptious slice of apple pie.

"Oh god, it looks so good," I said, digging into it with a fork. It felt amazing to finally be home and return to normal life as quickly as possible. I had everything in my life under control, and I needed it to go back that way.

"Your parents are thinking about going on vacation," said Grandma, leaning back in her rocking chair and taking a bite of the apple pie with her green tea.

"To where?"

"I think they said, *hawayy* or something like that," said Grandma.

I was confused for a moment.

"Do you mean Hawaii?"

"Yes," said Grandma. "It's amazing that omegas can travel now."

"But only with their alpha packs," I said, rolling my eyes, and she laughed out loud. The living room was getting darker, so I got up and flipped on the light switch. As I made my way back to the chair, I noticed Grandma staring at my neck.

I braced myself for her question.

"How did you get that mark?" she asked, with her mouth full.

"It's nothing," I said.

"Don't expect me to believe it was some animal like you told everyone else today," said Grandma. "Tell me the truth, granddaughter."

"Well, you wouldn't believe me if I told you," I said, debating whether or not to tell. I knew she was lonely here and wasn't really close to anyone but me.

"Try me," she said.

"It was a vampire," I said simply. "He bit me on the neck."

"Don't play around," she warned. "Are you lying?"

"No, I'm not," I said, conveying honesty in my tone. I took another sip of the hot chocolate. "There's a whole freaking clan of them hiding in the mountains."

Her eyes nearly bugged out of their sockets.

"That's unbelievable," she said. "Vampires are believed to be no longer around. I may be a beta, but I'm not stupid. I've seen a lot growing up on Howl's Edge but not vampires. Tell me what happened to you."

"I didn't have my heat suppressants, so I went into heat," I said, without going into detail about what happened. "Then a vampire helped me escape and dropped me off at the heat clinic."

"Oh wow," said Grandma. "Don't ever tell a soul that you've seen vampires. And you need to cover up that bite mark tomorrow with makeup."

"Why?"

"If anyone ever finds out you were involved with a vampire, the punishment is death," said Grandma, fearfully. "Several years ago, way before any one of us was born, it is said that vampires would steal omegas and use them for their blood. If an omega willingly gave herself to a vampire, she was hanged for her crimes. There isn't anything documented about those creatures, and saying the word 'vampires' out loud is trouble as it is."

Oh, crap. I didn't know how serious this was.

"I'll be careful," I said, sipping the hot chocolate. "And I definitely won't tell a soul. It's something I want to forget about forever."

Then Grandma leaned forward in her chair, her eyes sparkling with curiosity.

"Tell me about them. What do they look like? How do they survive?"

And the rest of the evening passed with me telling her everything I could about their eating habits and how they lived. I was fearful of talking loudly, so we whispered in the living room through the night, like we were being watched.

Two Weeks Later

I was at my shop wiping down the counters with a feather duster. It was a quiet day today, with only a few customers shopping on a Monday. It was a great start to the week, and I was glad to see that nothing had gone awry with me being away. Grandma had handled things well, with the merchandise neatly put away.

As I worked, I tried not to think about what had happened to me and all the knotting I'd had within the past few days. It was time to forget about all that and concentrate on today. But for some reason, I would get lost in thought, constantly thinking about James and where he could be.

"Excuse me," said a customer, and I looked up from the other side of the counter.

"How can I help you?" I asked.

"I have a couple of questions about a piece," she said, walking towards a shelf. As I walked to follow her, a wave of nausea hit me, and I felt the bile rising to my mouth. I tapped Grandma on the shoulder, who was organizing the books.

"Can you please take care of that customer?" I said quickly. Then I rushed to the back of the shop to the bathroom, hurling into the toilet. I gasped for breath, vomiting some more.

Rinsing my mouth in the sink, I wondered if it was something I had eaten. I didn't feel like I had a stomach bug since the nauseous feeling had passed. Splashing water on my face, I looked into the tiny cloudy mirror at my reflection. My face was blotchy, and strands of my hair were loose from my ponytail. I had been feeling more tired recently for no reason, but I attributed it to being taken by several males last month. More than I could count.

But this was worrying. Not enough to set off alarm bells, though.

Later, Grandma met me in the backroom while I sat on a chair, dizzy and feeling sick.

"You don't look well," said Grandma, feeling my forehead. "No fever."

"I've been throwing up," I said, closing my eyes to steady the motion sickness that went through me. She looked worried, sliding over her chair to sit beside me and rubbing my back.

"Take a pregnancy test," she said.

My eyes snapped open in shock.

"There's no way," I said, placing a hand on my stomach. "The heat clinic uses protection."

What if Markus's dream came true, and a condom *did* break along the way? But if it wasn't the alphas...no, my mind couldn't go there. I couldn't be pregnant with a vampire's child. Or my grandma was jumping to conclusions. There was no way in hell that I was pregnant.

"It's good to be prepared," said Grandma. "I've learned my lesson hiding everything from your mother. She never knew she was an omega, and I hid that fact for a long time until she went into heat. Tiana wasn't prepared at all, and I cried many nights through my guilt. She would have had a choice of her alpha pack, but thankfully things turned out okay for her."

"Mom never told me," I said, surprised.

"She was trapped in the middle of the ocean with four alphas who could think of nothing but rutting her," said Grandma. My stomach twisted, and I suddenly remembered how I was violated when I was sixteen. The innocence that was taken away from me in one horrible night. "She didn't have a choice but to accept, or else she would die."

My head spun thinking of my poor mother lost and trapped on a ship. Clutching her stomach in pain from her heat. She would have understood me if I had confided in her instead of running away from home as a teen. Tears sprung to my eyes at how distant I treated her.

"I need to see Mom," I said, filled with an overwhelming desire to hug her.

"The point I'm trying to make is that you need to be prepared for anything that life throws at you," said Grandma. "Buy yourself a pregnancy test and take the rest of the day off, Alana. I will stay at the shop until closing."

"Are you sure you'll be okay?"

"I've run your shop for many days now, have I not?" she asked, winking at me.

"Of course, you did an amazing job taking care of the shop. See you later then, Grandma."

"Let's hope to moons you're not pregnant, or else things could get a lot more complicated," she said ominously.

Chapter 19

Alana

I sat on the toilet, holding the pregnancy test between my fingers.

Waiting and waiting.

My heart pounded harder with each minute passing. I couldn't believe I was even in this position at all. I was starting to regret the fateful day I went off to the beach after the barbeque, which was the last normal day in my life. I desperately stared at the pink strip in my hand, willing it to declare that I wasn't pregnant after all. I couldn't imagine being pregnant and having to run after a baby while running my shop. But if it was a vampire baby...

A word flashed across the screen, and my heart stopped. It said: *Pregnant*.

Fuck my life.

Breathing hard, I dropped the test in the trash and pulled up my underwear and jeans. I washed my hands in a trance-like state. This couldn't be happening to me. Not like this. Would the baby grow up without a father?

Leaving the bathroom, I walked down my grandma's hallway and into my room. My room was simple- a bed in the middle draped covered in blue sheets and a white fur rug on the ground. After closing the door behind me, I kicked off my sneakers and flopped onto the bed, lying on my side. I placed a hand on my belly, imagining the life growing within me. My heart hadn't stopped racing, and I tried to take deep calming breaths.

I would figure something out. I had to.

I didn't realize I had fallen asleep until I heard a knock at the door.

"Come in," I said groggily, rubbing my eyes. I looked at the clock, which said eight p.m. I couldn't believe I had slept for so long, but I was up at seven in the morning to work, which explained my tiredness.

I sat up in the bed, and upon seeing Grandma walk into the room, the memory of the test came to my mind. Dread filled my entire being, unable to believe I'd come to this point. I was such a disappointment of a granddaughter.

She sat on the bed beside me, still wearing her purple apron from the shop.

"So what did the test say?" she asked eagerly, clasping her hands on her lap.

"I'm pregnant."

"What?!" she squealed, her hands on her face in shock.

"Yes," I said, shaking my head. "Sorry, Grandma."

"Listen," she said, grasping my hands. "There's nothing you can do about this now but to accept it. Your baby will be loved, and there's a whole family waiting for the baby. You don't need a traditional alpha pack to care for you."

"But there's something else," I said, my throat closing from emotion. "The baby might not be from Lio and his pack."

"What are you saying?"

"I slept with the vampire," I said. "It could be a vampire baby."

"You never told me you slept with that vampire," admonished Grandma. "So we don't know for sure whether the baby is one of us or half-vampire?"

"Yes," I said, staring at my laundry basket across the room.

"It's not your fault, my dear," she said in a kinder voice. "But for now, we need to keep this a secret until the day you give birth. If the baby is half-vampire, you and our entire family could be executed."

"What?!"

"Even though it's not spoken about now, no one on the island will be happy about this."

"Wouldn't I need to go to the hospital to give birth? How about all the checkups?"

"You need to stay hidden. Once in a while, we can ask Dr. Keera to take a look at you. You cannot go to a hospital under any circumstances," ordered Grandma.

Shit. My head was spinning with all of this. The panic was settling over me.

"Where the hell would I give birth?"

"We will figure that out when we get to it," said Grandma, standing up. "I need to make a few phone calls. But for now, we must pretend nothing happened. Just work at your shop and come home. No hanging out with friends or anything for nine months. Got it?"

"Got it," I said in a low voice as she left the room.

My life as I knew it was completely over.

Five Months Later

For a while, I had been able to hide my pregnancy. Well...until today.

I was at my shop - high up on the ladder organizing the yarn supply on the top shelf. It had been a busier day at the shop, and opening boxes in the backroom was tiring me out.

I got more anxious as each day passed.

I still hadn't seen a doctor, and I had no idea how the baby was doing. I wasn't taking any chances despite Grandma wanting to get Dr. Keera involved, but I reminded her that Keera would just tell her son Lio. And that stopped her right away.

Grandma was busy ringing up items at the front for a few customers. I made a mental note to check if she needed help after I arranged the yarn by color.

"Lana?" said a familiar voice from below the ladder, and my heart jumped.

A voice that I hadn't heard in a while.

I looked down, seeing the familiar swoop of his black hair over his eye and the tilt of his head. I wasn't expecting to see Lio here, and I nearly fell down the ladder. I quickly straightened my large shirt so he couldn't see the outline of my small but growing belly. I didn't know how I felt about seeing him, so I stepped down a couple of steps instead of getting off the ladder entirely so he knew I was busy.

I still hadn't forgiven him for the way he stormed out on me when

I was at the heat clinic.

"What's up, Lio?" I asked in a stern voice, keeping one hand on the ladder and one on my hips. Conveying my annoyance quite clearly.

"Hey Lana, I just wanted to apologize," he said, leaning his hand against the shelf, caging me between his arms. His head came up to my belly, and I realized I had stopped on the steps at the worst spot. I tried to regulate my breathing. Then he pulled out a bouquet of roses. "I wasn't sure what color you liked, so I got red roses because you liked red fireworks. But here you go."

"Why? Why are you apologizing now?" I asked him, confused. I didn't know how I felt about him being here, and at the same time, I wanted him here too. For some reason, I felt a bit of comfort in his presence. *Was it because he was the first alpha to ever knot me?* I wasn't sure.

"I kept calling you Lana," he insisted. "On my days off, I'd come over here, but it would only be your grandma around. Or you'd be hiding in the back."

It was true.

I *had* been ignoring his calls like there was no tomorrow and avoiding him. I needed to protect myself, my family, and my future baby.

"Sorry," I said. "I was busy."

"So today, I called out of work to be here," he said, handing me the bouquet of roses. Bending over to grab it, I gripped the stems and set the roses on an empty spot on the shelf. I planned to give it to Grandma, who'd have some use for it later.

"I'm sure it was tough calling out of work and leaving an omega in distress," I said. I regretted it as soon as I said it. I *was* jealous, but he didn't need to know that. Imagining him knotting some other omega made my stomach roil.

"Lana, what's that smell?" he asked, poking his nose against my belly. "It's your scent but bitter."

"Well, I've been working hard all day," I said hastily, trying to pull away, but my back hit the ladder instead. Then he suddenly pressed his ear against my belly. I tried to push his head away, but he immediately looked at me, face white.

"Lana," he growled. "Are you pregnant?"

"I..."

"Don't you dare lie to me."

A customer in line turned to look at us, and my face heated. Lio wasn't supposed to know that I was pregnant.

"Yes," I said in a low voice so the customer could mind their own business again. "It's not yours or anything, so it's nothing to worry about."

"How many months?" he said, wrapping his fingers around my thigh. "How many months pregnant are you?"

"Five, gosh," I said, taken aback by his intensity. If I were him, I'd leave little old me to raise a child alone and not be worried about it. Just go on by and continue fucking omegas in heat.

I could see the look in his eyes as he quickly calculated when I was at the heat clinic. It was the same day I slept with James. There was no way to know, and I couldn't tell him either. His eyes widened as he stared at my face.

"Then it could be mine or my pack's," he said. "Most likely, Markus used a bad condom or purposely pinched the tip of it. Either way, the baby is ours."

Oh, shit. Things were moving way too quickly.

"What if it isn't?" I said, stalling for time before he jumped to conclusions.

"I know you Alana," said Lio. "You would never have come to the heat clinic if you didn't have a mate."

"But someone brought me there," I hinted. "And I don't remember what happened."

His face fell for a moment then a resolved look came over him.

"Either way, I will be the one to protect you and take you as my omega," said Lio. "My team's contract is over now that we've accidentally gotten you pregnant. I'm no longer employed there and will never return there regardless, even if the baby isn't mine."

"Lio, no, don't quit your job," I said, climbing down the last few steps of the ladder. I was nervous of where his train of thought was going. He wanted me to be his omega, but we weren't there yet at all. "I don't want to be together just because there's a baby."

He pulled out his cell phone, ready to call the heat clinic. He slowly lowered his arm, staring at me incredulously.

"Do you really think I want you as my omega just because you're pregnant? I've always loved you, and you know this, Lana."

My heart was pumping hard. I knew it in my soul that he did.

Chapter 20

Alana

J ust then, Grandma interrupted us and pulling me by the arm.

"Excuse us, Lio. I need to speak to my granddaughter for a minute," she said to him, and he nodded tersely. Once I was in the back stockroom with my grandma, I panicked.

"He *knows* I'm pregnant," I said. "And he wants to take me as his omega. I'm going to refuse him, though or run away and hide."

"Wait, wait," said Grandma slowly. "If the baby is his, then there's no problem? The baby will not be fatherless."

"Yes, but if it isn't, then I'm taking a huge risk," I whispered. "We could all be in massive trouble, and all of us executed."

"I trust that he will keep you safe either way," Grandma whispered back harshly. She grabbed me by the shoulders. "This is actually good. Let him keep you as his omega so everyone knows you're pregnant and in love before you start to show. If you don't accept his offer, you'll be the talk of the island, the rejected omega with no pack."

"But Grandma," I sighed, shaking my head. "This is a bad idea. I don't even know Lio that much, and do you remember what he did as a job?"

"Alphas change," said Grandma. "They change for their omega. We had him waiting for a while now though. Let's go back."

When we walked back to the front of the shop, leaving the stockroom, I was shocked to see Markus and Owen also there, with Lio standing in the middle of them. Markus had a wide smile on his face and Owen looked stunned as he gazed at my belly.

"We need to talk," said Lio, whose arms were crossed.

"I'll take care of the customers," whispered Grandma. "All of you can talk in the backroom over there."

My heart was pounding hard, and I was getting dizzy from all the activity surrounding my pregnancy. It was getting way out of hand with the amount of people knowing. If I was indeed carrying a vampire's baby, I needed to go into hiding as soon as possible. Once we were in the backroom, I stood facing all three of them, who looked at me expectantly.

"Will you be our omega?" Markus blurted out, and Owen punched him on the arm.

"That's not how you woo an omega, you oaf," said Owen.

"Are you really pregnant?" asked Markus, coming over to touch my belly. I allowed him because I felt a weird close bond with Markus and Owen. Something about working with them during my heat caused the attachment to form.

"I am," I said, loving how his large hand caressed my belly. It had been a while since anyone had touched me like that. And it felt good. Tears sprung to my eyes as they all watched me. *Stupid hormones*.

"Lana, what's wrong?" asked Lio, stepping over to me and placing a hand on the small of my back. He leaned his face down to my shoulder, his hot breath brushing my neck. "Don't cry."

"This is not real, your feelings for me. None of it is," I cried.

He wrapped his fingers around mine, pulling my palm to his chest.

"Nothing is more real to me than the feelings I have for you," he said, and that's when I really believed him. The tearful joy in his eyes when he said that, or it was the sincerity in his voice. "I have never felt for any omega except for you in all my years of working at the heat clinic. My entire life, I've wanted you, Lana. Will you not push me away this time?"

I breathed in and out, aware that the outline of my breasts was showing too much in this huge grey shirt of mine. I was scared to give them an answer. My heart wanted to be with them. To have a pack. But my brain was screaming at me to run and hide.

"I don't want to push you away," I said. "But it would take a lot more than flowers to apologize for how you treated me at the heat clinic."

"I know," said Lio, pressing his lips to my cheek, kissing away my tear. I turned to face him, and our lips met.

Our first kiss.

We had our first kiss in the cramped stockroom full of boxes, with two other males watching. My eyes closed on their own accord, feeling how his lips moved over mine as Markus whistled.

"Nice," said Owen. It was all background noise to me as I melted into Lio's arms when he pulled me close. His sideburns brushed my face as he deepened the kiss. Our lips moved as one, feeling and tasting each other at long last. Ever since we were young, I wanted him to kiss me like this.

To pull me close in his strong arms and make me feel safe.

"We can continue this at home," said Lio.

"Home?" I said, a little taken aback at how fast this was moving.

His lips twitched. "Wouldn't you be moving in with us? Your new pack?"

My mind was racing.

I wasn't sure if I felt all these warm fuzzy feelings because of the kiss, but I needed to sort my thoughts out about this entire thing. Especially if I was going to have a half-vampire baby, I needed to buy some time.

"Umm, give me at least a few days to pack. How about on Thursday?"

"I can help you pack," offered Owen, his eyes hopeful, but Lio calmly placed a hand on his shoulder.

"No Owen. We will let her pack her things. Just call me when you're ready," said Lio, trying not to scare me off by the intensity of his pack, and I appreciated it. I did need some space and wasn't about to move in with them at the drop of a hat.

"Thank you," I said. "There's no need for us to rush things at all."

But the few days seemed to pass quicker than I thought it would. I was sitting on my grandma's couch as I watched Markus, Owen, and Lio haul my boxes to the trunk of their van. My grandma was sitting next to me, holding a book in her hand and a cup of tea in the other.

"The boys are doing a fantastic job. They're almost done," she observed over her glasses.

"They're moving too quickly," I said.

"Just as they should for their omega."

146

"It's a good thing Mom and them are out on vacation," I said. "I wouldn't know how to explain this."

"I'm going to miss having you around my child."

"Hey, don't say that," I said, my eyes burning with unshed tears. "We'll see each other around at the shop. This isn't goodbye."

"You're right, I'm just being dramatic," said Grandma, setting down her tea and blowing her nose. Markus came up to us and sat next to my grandma.

"We'll take extra good care of your granddaughter," he said gruffly, expressing his honesty and commitment. Even though I've only known Markus for a short time, I believed him. He was a good alpha at heart, despite his gruff exterior.

"I understand," sniffled Grandma.

"Are you ready to come with us?" asked Markus, and I nodded as I bit the inside of my cheek.

Was I doing the right thing?

I hugged Grandma, willing myself not to burst into tears. I stared at the vase of roses on the kitchen counter while I hugged her.

My heart pounded hard when Markus took my hand and led me to the door. Lio and Owen were already in the van by the time we reached them, with Owen in the driver's seat. I hated change in my life, but this was really happening. Every step of the way. I was only doing this for my baby.

For my baby to have a loving family and fathers who loved him.

As I settled into the backseat of the car between Markus and Lio, I leaned back against the chair and massaged the tense muscles in my belly.

"Lana," said Lio to my right, and I turned to look at him. "Don't

147

be sad. You'll get used to your new life very soon, and with a new baby on the way, you'll never be lonely."

I nodded silently. If I talked, I might cry.

Markus silently put his arm around my shoulders, and I leaned into him. He started purring with the deep, strong vibrations in his chest, which flowed throughout my body like a life current.

Calming my mind and my soul.

Chapter 21

Four Months Later

Alana

Waking up between alphas every morning was something I wasn't used to, but it felt good.

Markus's arm was draped over my thigh while he snored behind me in bed, and Lio's hand cradled the top of my head while he slept. Owen liked to sleep in his own room after our nightly group activities. He claimed he loved his sleep, and no one was going to ruin it for him.

I carefully rolled onto my back, trying not to squish Markus's arm. At nine months pregnant, my belly had extended far beyond what I could handle. I rubbed my eyes and watched the rain pit-patter against the window on this gloomy day. Ever since I had moved into their house, the pack was careful with me and patient with everything they did with me. It had taken two weeks for me to sleep in the same room as them.

I smiled at the memory of my family meeting Lio and his pack when I first moved in. They were excited for me, especially my little sisters. Adam didn't have much to say except *'congrats sis'*. But still, no one knew I was pregnant and I asked Lio not to tell anyone. For the last four months after the introductions, I had kept to myself, hiding away at home.

Never leaving the house.

They couldn't know. No one was allowed to know.

Lio, Markus, and Owen were sure the baby was theirs because I hadn't told them about my time with James. I was too scared they'd go after him and kill him along with all his people. Or even kill *me* and dispose of my body somewhere in the ocean, which I was starting to doubt by the love they've shown me every day. They had each taken up different hobbies after the heat clinic compensated them for the accidental pregnancy.

I got off the bed, and the heated hardwood floor was warm on my feet as I walked to the bathroom naked. The best part about moving out of Grandma's house was walking around naked and being desired by my pack. After brushing my teeth, I took a relaxing shower, thinking about what I would do when it was time to give birth. The pack respected my decision about not going to the hospital, but they were getting antsy as the time drew nearer. The warm water slowly woke me up as I rubbed my hand over my pregnant belly. Over the last couple of days, I would get small contractions but nothing too severe.

After my shower, I wrapped myself in a bathrobe with my hair wet around my shoulders. I slipped my feet into fuzzy warm slippers and headed downstairs to make coffee.

It was nine in the morning, but the men woke up late since quitting their jobs at the heat clinic. They were finally relaxing. But the downside was that they had a lot of pent-up sexual energy to give me ever since they quit. They were used to being on-call at anytime several times a day. At one point, I had woken up to Markus licking my pussy in the middle of the night, and I spread my legs further for him half-asleep, riding my orgasm against his mouth while he slurped.

As I navigated the kitchen, I placed a hand on my belly, feeling the baby move restlessly. My heart glowed with contentment. I already loved the baby more than anything, and even if the baby turned out to be a vampire, I would still love him. A feeling of emptiness still resided in me without my first love, James, but I would have to live without him.

"Ah, there you are," said Lio, pressing up behind me and cupping my breasts. "I was a little worried about you."

I smiled at the raw expression of emotion and leaned my head against his hard chest.

"Why were you worried?" I teased as he kissed my hair.

"Anything could happen. Some jerk could break in and rape you."

I froze, and his eyebrows rose with concern.

"Um."

"Did I say something, Alana?" asked Lio. He still had no idea what happened to me.

"Why would they do that when you're sleeping right next to me?" I joked, hoping to lighten the tension.

"Shh, Lana, you're talking too much," said Lio, kissing me on the lips. "I can never be too careful with you."

"Even with all your surveillance cameras all around this massive house?"

"Even then," he said, smoothing my hair back from my shoulders. "You've showered and everything. You prepared for a good fucking, didn't you? I can't wait to lick that nice shiny pussy."

"Who said fucking?" said Markus, whose footsteps were rushing towards us, and I laughed.

"No one is," I said loudly. "We're going to have breakfast like a nice normal family."

Then Lio lifted me onto the counter, and I squealed. I was no match for his sheer alpha strength.

"I'm way too big for this!" I said. "Plus, it's not safe."

"Fuck, I wasn't thinking," said Lio with a sparkle in his eyes. "Don't worry, I've seen pregnant people lift weights."

"The alpha females?"

"Omegas can do it too," he said, spreading my bathrobe apart to reveal my naked thighs.

"I need to make breakfast," I protested.

"I will have my breakfast right here, thank you very much," he grunted, kissing my thighs aggressively and softly biting my skin. "Lean back for me so I can lick your tight little cunt."

Markus joined us in the kitchen, freshly washed as he kissed me on the lips, helping me lean back as my bathrobe cushioned my elbows. Lio started spreading my legs, and I felt a rush of warmth between my legs, my pussy coming alive as he gazed deeply.

"How will you reach my pussy? My stomach's too big."

He lifted my legs over his shoulders and pulled my ass to the edge of the counter in one swift move while Markus held me by the hips.

"Does that answer your question?" he asked with one eyebrow raised. My pussy just inches from his mouth.

"Yes," I gasped when I felt his rough tongue swipe my entire pussy in one giant lick.

"I want pussy breakfast, too," said Markus, settling his face between

152

my legs from the top.

"You can take her clit then," said Lio.

My pussy clenched with arousal, unable to wait for them to start on their breakfast. I heard the shower going on upstairs from Owen.

With Markus's arm underneath my back and wrapped around me protectively, he dipped his head once again between my legs. I felt his tongue slide around my clit, hitting all my erogenous zones. I bucked against his tongue, and Lio stuck his own tongue deep into my vagina. I couldn't control it as slick dripped from me, and Lio would lap it up with his tongue.

I moaned as I felt both tongues licking and prodding my pussy constantly until I kept releasing slick.

"More, sweetheart," groaned Markus.

I stared at our reflection in the living room mirror. Lio's head was between my separated legs, with my feet sticking above his shoulders. And Markus was leaning across my belly and licking furiously.

"More?" I gasped when another stream of slick went down my thighs. Markus's lips captured my clit as he started to suck. "Oh!"

I gripped Markus's hair in desperation, shuddering under their tongues. I tried to close my legs, but Lio spread them wider, trapping my pussy with their tongues. They persisted in licking, sucking, and prodding harder. Licking in swirls and adding pressure until I sobbed through my moans.

"So fucking delicious," said Lio, sucking my pussy. "Look at how her cunt is dripping all over the floor."

"Shiny and sweet," growled Markus, softly licking my sensitive clit. "So fuckable, aren't you, baby?"

"Yes," I moaned while they cleaned me up after my earth-shattering orgasm. "I can't even move right now. I feel like jello."

"Perfect," said Lio, pulling down his pants. He pressed his cock against my dripping slit, and I breathed faster as he did that. "I think Markus is right. It's time to fuck you, isn't that right, baby?"

"Yes, please, alpha," I said, taking in his huge cock as he pushed himself in deeper. My eyes rolled back in pleasure as he started to thrust. Markus was kissing my neck, nibbling me as Lio pumped into me.

Lio's hand stroked my pregnant belly, watching my face as he fucked me on the kitchen counter.

"My cock feels snug and tight inside your pussy right now," said Lio. "I never want to stop."

"Then don't stop," I gasped as he thrust harder and faster into me. He grunted with each thrust and each slap of his balls against my ass.

"Fuck," he shouted when he reached his climax. Spurts of hot liquid shot into me, filling me as he came. "Oh fuck, I love knotting you raw."

Without a condom, the knottings were more intense and felt so much hotter. When he knotted inside me, I moaned from how good it felt.

We were one at this moment.

"Are we stuck in this kitchen now?" I asked with a smile.

"Don't worry, baby," said Lio, carrying me to the living room with my legs wrapped around his waist while he was deep inside me. My limbs were trembling, and my pussy was throbbing from all this morning's attention. We laid on the couch for a half hour, talking about improvements to my store and baby names.

When his knot finally released me, I sat up and hastily tied my bathrobe around me before they got any other ideas. Sometimes we were incapable of doing anything but fucking all day. But today, they had a long-awaited speedboat trip with another alpha pack.

"Aren't you supposed to be getting ready to go?" I said. Markus was pouring the coffee into cups in the kitchen.

"With you being so close to giving birth, I don't think it's a good idea," said Lio.

"Listen, it could be another two weeks," I insisted. And I'd rather not have them here if I gave birth to a half-vampire baby. "I'm perfectly fine. I'll just snuggle up on the couch here and order food. No big deal."

"Are you sure, baby?" Lio asked, rubbing my back. Owen finally appeared in the living room, and he smiled when he saw me. His hair was gelled back, and he was wearing a windbreaker and jeans.

"I'm very sure, Lio," I said.

"Why aren't you big slow alphas getting ready?" asked Owen, bounding down the steps. "We have a big day ahead of us."

"Alright then," said Lio, slowly tearing himself away from me after giving me one last kiss. "I'll get ready then."

Lio left the living room to get ready, and Owen looked at me. My hair was out of place, and it looked it like he knew what had happened.

"Yes, we knotted," I admitted before he could ask.

"Thought so," he said. "Can I at least look at your pussy? I want to see all the cream they left in you."

"Do you have to, Owen?" I whined. I didn't want to get the males riled up again.

"Yes, or else I'd have to fuck you before leaving, sweetheart," said Owen. "I know you want to get rid of us today."

"Okay, fine," I said, untying my bathrobe.

"Spread your legs," said Owen with an evil gleam in his eyes.

I leaned back on the couch and lifted my right thigh over the armrest of the couch.

"Do you see now?" I asked.

"That's the perfect view," he breathed, kneeling before me and watching Lio's cum drip down my butt. With his gaze focused on my pussy, he caught a drip of the liquid with his finger, stuffing it back inside me. "We can't let it go to waste."

"Oh," I said as he pressed his finger into my pussy. "You're making me horny again."

"Sorry sweet thing," he said, popping his finger out with a loud squelch. "Your pussy looks nice and stretched with your alpha's semen leaking. I wish I had time to bathe you."

True to my word, I relaxed on the couch watching a heartbreaking romance movie about an omega who couldn't be with the pack she wanted. I blew my nose into a tissue as I munched on popcorn. Pausing the movie, I realized that the house had gotten dark and night had fallen. I slowly got up and wobbled to the light switch, flipping on all the lights before it got too creepy.

But when I returned to the couch, my stomach suddenly cramped up in pain. I held onto the armrest for balance. I gritted my teeth, waiting for the contraction to pass. I took a couple of deep breaths, just as I'd seen my mom do when she had my sisters. When the band of the contraction released me, I was sweating profusely.

Oh, my moons.

That was intense.

I tried to take another step to the couch, but a second wave of pain squeezed my belly, and a rush of liquid expelled between my legs. *Oh no.* This wasn't good at all. I looked at the empty tub in the living room that the alphas had prepared for my water birth, but it was too late. I needed to get to my phone and call Grandma. I pressed my bathrobe between my legs to dry things up a little bit.

The baby was coming tonight.

Chapter 22

Alana

I leaned against the couch as I slowly walked around it, my face scrunched in pain.

I hoped I could at least get to my phone on the table before another contraction seized me. But right before I reached the table, my belly squeezed in pain like a rubber band around my waist. I took three deep breaths feeling a heaviness drop between my legs.

Oh my god.

I was so stupid for letting Lio go like that. Even if the baby was half-vampire, Lio would accept us. I couldn't imagine him throwing us out. When the contraction released me, I quickly reached out for my phone, grasping it tightly. I dialed Grandma's number and put it on speaker.

"Hello," she said. "I can't hear you. Hello."

"Grandma, it's me," I said breathlessly. "Can you hear me?"

"Yes, dear. What is..."

"I'm about to have the baby! The pack aren't here right now," I said. "I need your help."

"Oh my, are you serious?"

"If it's a vampire baby, we need to go into hiding," I said quickly, my words tumbling over each other.

"I'm coming," said Grandma.

Another contraction squeezed me as I hung up.

I yelled and grunted in pain. I leaned against the birthing ball, which helped ease some of the pain. This hurt way more than I thought it would. I never expected the pain to be so intense and unforgiving.

"I can't do this," I groaned to myself when the pain finally released me. The contractions were only seconds apart, and the heaviness between my legs increased. I pressed a hand between my legs and felt hair.

The baby's head was there.

My blood ran cold as I leaned against the ball in shock. The baby was coming right now. I lay on the floor on my back, and it felt like a balloon stretching below me, ready to burst. The pain was incredible. My breaths came out in gasps as I cradled the baby's head with my hand and pushed. I gritted my teeth and screamed in pain. It felt like every inch of skin was ripping down there.

I heard the front door open.

"In here!" I screamed.

Heavy footsteps ran towards me, and I opened my eyes to see Lio, Markus, and Owen with horrified expressions on their faces seeing me on the ground like this.

"She's having the fucking baby," said Markus.

"I knew we should have taken her to the hospital!" screamed Owen.

"Owen, grab blankets," said Lio, going into professional mode right away while I screamed in agony as the baby's head came out further. Lio knelt between my legs with serious determination on his face. "Markus, get scissors and boiling water to disinfect. Then purr into her when you're back. The calming effect will make this easier on her and open her up."

"It hurts," I moaned.

"I know, baby," said Lio. His calming voice reassured me that all wasn't as dreadful and horrifying as I thought. It felt like my entire world was going to collapse within minutes of giving birth if the baby wasn't Lio's. He would know immediately if the baby wasn't his. "Push Lana."

I took a deep breath and pushed with all my might. The pain between my legs was unbearable as I screamed.

"Again," said Lio calmingly. "You're doing great, baby."

"Listen to him, sweetheart," said my grandmother's voice. I looked up and locked eyes with her. Only she knew my secret.

"What if something happens?" I cried out. Her eyes flashed. She knew what I was talking about.

"You will be strong if anything happens," she said firmly- in a suck-it-up tone of voice. "You are a strong omega, and you can survive anything. Go ahead and listen to your alpha. Push like you mean it."

I took another deep breath and bore down with all my strength. I would have this baby, and I would love him or her.

No matter what.

I gritted my teeth and pushed again, my screams echoing throughout the house. When I heard the baby's cries, my heart beat faster, and tears streamed down my face. My baby was here.

"There she is," said Lio when the baby plopped onto his arms. He handed the baby to Markus. "Markus, wipe her face down."

I screamed again in pain when I felt a second heaviness press down my vagina.

Twins?

"Another one!" shouted Markus in excitement.

"Hold my hand," said Owen, and I grabbed his hand as I pushed again while Lio peered between my legs. The baby slid right out in the next couple of seconds, and the pain finally dissipated.

"This one is a boy. Here you go," he said to my grandma.

I collapsed against the ground, my eyes shut tight as I heard the babies crying. My body was weak in all the places, and my pussy hurt so bad as Lio cleaned me up. After a few minutes, I opened my eyes to see everyone staring at the crying babies in silence.

"What? What's wrong?" I asked, my heart sinking.

"There's something..." said Lio slowly as he stared at the baby in Grandma's hands.

"The boy doesn't look normal," said Markus in a shocked voice.

"Why the fuck are you scaring Alana?" said Owen loudly as he quickly made his way to the babies. "Oh, my god."

I shut my eyes tight, breathing hard. Then I sat up in a pool of my bloody mess and stared at the baby in my grandmother's hands, who was squirming, wrapped in a blanket. He had stark red eyes and nearly translucent skin.

The baby looked exactly like the vampires in the secret city. An exact replica of James but with my facial features. The girl baby in Markus's arms looked normal without the omega mark on her shoulder. The omega mark was three small claw marks on every omega's shoulders, signifying that she belonged to a pack. My baby girl could be either a beta or an alpha female, but I wouldn't be sure until she had grown.

"What is this?" said Lio, blinking rapidly and staunching my bleeding with a cloth. "How is this possible? The man who dropped you off at the clinic. He was a vampire wasn't he?"

Tears streamed down my face as I nodded, crying.

This was the worst-case scenario, and I thought all of it was behind me. I didn't even want to look at the babies. My heart was beating so fast that I thought I might pass out.

"Be patient," advised my grandmother gently.

Lio exhaled after a moment. "Listen, I need a moment, okay? She lied to all of us. I don't know who to fucking trust now." He washed his hands in the kitchen, walking out of the house, and my heart felt like it was torn into a million pieces.

I tried to get up, but Owen pressed a hand to my chest.

"Don't. We'll take care of you," he said, his eyes darting wildly between the vampire baby and me like he couldn't believe what was happening.

"I'm so sorry," I said weakly, getting up on my elbows. I was in excruciating pain, and I was getting dizzy. "I should have told you."

"It's okay," said Owen, scooping me up in his arms. "Let's get all this blood washed off you and take care of you. I would drive you to the hospital immediately, but I can't because they'll want to see the babies. Stay with me, Alana."

I struggled not to let the dizziness overtake me as my head bounced on his arm.

"Owen," I said.

"Don't, it's okay," he insisted, rushing me up the stairs. "Relax, baby. Just relax."

He sat me down in the bathtub and removed my bathrobe.

I was too scared to look down there and see the mess. I knew it was messy from all the blood all over his arms. The bathtub was cold underneath me until he turned on the water. I couldn't focus as he poured the water over me, scrubbing my skin. My eyes burned with tears and soon I was crying uncontrollably while he washed me, my tears mixing in with the water and blood. Owen pressed kisses on my head while he washed my back and legs.

"It's all my fault," I blubbered. "Lio is leaving because of me."

"He'll never leave you," reassured Owen. "Don't cry baby."

"The baby...isn't his," I hiccupped, feeling like I was going to faint.

"I need you to relax. Now," commanded Owen. I looked up at him when he used that sharp tone. He was never rough with me like that. "I don't want you blaming yourself and making yourself weaker baby. You have to be strong for your babies."

"How?!" I yelled through my pain and tears. "How will I go on living like this?"

"Shh, take a deep breath baby," said Owen and I inhaled. "Another one."

I took another deep breath still in shock. How would I feed my baby boy? Would he drink milk? James hated all the normal food I ate. Fear and terror flowed through me, worsening with every minute passing by. Everything passed by in slow motion, by the time Owen dried me up, placed a pad in my new underwear, and tucked me in my bed with blankets all around me. He was the best when it came to taking care of me.

"Why are you so nice to me?" I asked exhausted from my tears, leaning against the headboard as I watched my grandma and Markus enter the room with the freshly washed babies. The baby in Markus's arms was crying uncontrollably.

"I care about you, Alana. And so does the rest of us," he said, tucking in the blankets around my legs.

I looked away from the babies, terrified to hold the vampire one.

"Sweetheart dear, time to meet your babies," said Grandma. "You need to feed your little boy."

I froze. I couldn't do it. Tears blurred my eyes as I stared at the blankets, hearing his cries.

"I can't," I muttered. From the side of my eye, I saw Markus walking to the side of the bed, and then he put a weight between my arms. The baby stopped crying, and I was scared to look.

"Little omega, look at your baby," said Markus gruffly. "He loves you already. He knows your voice."

The tears fell harder, my heart heavy as Owen dabbed my face with a tissue.

I finally turned my head to look.

The baby's eyes were a calmer shade of red now, his little mouth opening and closing in a sucking motion. He was like a little bird, searching for food as he pressed his mouth against my arm. His pale face was so small, and I stared at him in wonder and amazement.

My heart grew ten sizes, wanting to feed and take care of this baby that I pushed out on my own.

Right now, no one matter but my baby. Not Lio, not anyone.

"Hush, baby Jay," I whispered, kissing his little cheek, and he cooed upon the skin contact. I pulled my blanket down, exposing my breast to feed him.

"What if he drinks blood?" muttered Markus.

The baby latched onto me, sucking with his tiny bird lips.

"Oh, it's painful," I said, gritting my teeth as he sucked. It felt like the milk was straining to come out, burning within me.

"It will get easier, I promise, dear," said Grandma, cooing at the little girl in her arms. "You're doing so good, Alana. I'm so proud of you."

Chapter 23

Lio

As I paced around the driveway, my brain was in shambles. This was unfixable. She betrayed and lied to me.

This omega had no problem lying to me since the day I found out she was pregnant. *How the fuck did she keep a straight face the entire time? Did she think this was a joke?*

I fumed as I sat in my car and leaned my head against the steering wheel.

"Fuck!" I yelled, banging my head against the headrest.

There was no way we would make this work.

Did she even have real feelings the entire time I touched her? Or was this a ploy for me to take care of her?

I needed to know the truth. I needed to know how she ended up in this situation and if this vampire violated her. If she was violated, I was going to kill him. But if she willingly slept with him....that was punishable by law.

I took a few deep breaths before getting out of my car. Alana needed my help in a time like this. I walked into the house, not seeing anyone in the living room. They must have all gone upstairs.

I cleaned up the mess on the hardwood floor, taking out some of my frustrations. I was sweating bullets as I washed my hands and splashed my face with cold water. I could hear one of the babies upstairs crying, and my heart wrenched with pain for Alana. We needed to give the vampire baby to his father, and that was it. Or else we would all be executed if she kept the baby.

When I walked into the room shortly after, there was silence except for the sounds of the baby girl suckling on Alana's breast. The second baby was sleeping soundly between Alana and Owen in the middle of the bed. Markus stood protectively over Alana with his arms crossed as he glared at me. Her grandmother was fussing with the mess in the room, picking up various things here and there. But everyone stopped as they stared at me walking in.

The tension in the room was heavy.

My eyes met Alana's, and I could see the tired lines on her face. Her dark hair tumbled around her bare shoulders, her eyes puffy and exhausted from her tears. God, she was so beautiful even when she wasn't all dolled up. She had a natural beauty that I adored and loved. She was *my* omega.

"Stay right over there," said Markus, immediately blocking her from sight.

"I'm not going to do anything," I reassured him.

"It's okay, Markus," said Alana in a small voice.

Markus rubbed his beard and grunted, moving aside for me. I neared the bed and carefully sat on the edge of it as she watched me. I didn't want to startle her. But she still flinched when I came near, and that pained me.

"I'm not angry, Lana," I said, trying to reassure her. "I just want to know. What happened?"

"She's tired, Lio," said Owen sharply. Even though he was a beta, he was a tough one when it came to the comfort of omegas. The vampire baby on the bed started to cry, and Grandma Bianca swiftly picked him up, rocking him as she walked around the room.

Alana sighed, looking up from the baby she was breastfeeding.

"The man who you saw in the surveillance video," she said. "He's the father of these babies."

"An actual vampire?" I said, my voice incredulous. But I had seen the baby with my own eyes, so I knew she wasn't lying. "Tell me what happened before I hunt him down and kill him."

"Please don't," she said, her voice rising and her chest heaving with panic. Something told me she cared deeply about this person, which didn't sit well with me.

"Shh, relax. Lio won't do anything," said Markus bending down and kissing her head. "Not while I'm here."

"Tell me what happened," I said, licking my lips. Prepared for anything.

"Well, it was all my fault when I went looking for him," she said hesitantly.

"Why in the hell were you looking for him?"

"Do you remember the campfire day when we were in high school?" she asked.

"Yes, I never forgot," I said. "The first time you broke my heart and disappeared that night."

"I...," she started to say but then clammed up. She looked around at everyone in the room nervously.

"You can say whatever is on your mind," said Owen, wrapping an arm around her.

"When I walked away from the campfire, four boys followed me," she whispered, and my heart sunk in my chest.

"What did they do to you?"

"One of them, he...raped me," she said in a low voice. I shut my eyes tight in horror. She had gone through that while I sat angrily in my tent, waiting for her that night. The room was silent as we took in the shocking statement. "Then the vampire showed up and stopped them. If he hadn't, I wouldn't know where I would be."

She only disappeared because she was scared of what I would think. *She was attacked.*

"I'm so fucking sorry," I said, my throat catching. I cleared my throat and scooted close to her. Owen moved aside for me, and I hugged her from the side while she silently rested her head on my chest. We both watched the baby girl feeding from her. The baby's eyes were closed and her button nose looking exactly like Alana's. "So that's why you went looking for the vampire. Did he do the same thing to you then?"

"It wasn't the same," she said vehemently, shaking her head. "His people forced him to."

"So it was the same thing," I said, my voice rising. "It was force, not love."

"But I love him," she said, her voice trembling.

"What?"

I couldn't believe what she had just said. It was a complete and utter betrayal of our kind. For an omega to fall in love with a different species and not her fated alphas was unheard of.

"You wouldn't understand," she said, shaking her head. "His people wanted me dead, but he wouldn't allow it. I went into heat, and he risked his own life for me. He ran away and brought me to you to save my life."

Chills went through me. *If he betrayed his own people for her...*only a fated mate would do that.

"He must have had strong feelings for you," I said, slightly jealous. "Now you're in extreme danger if you keep your vampire baby."

"I know," she said, sighing. "I don't know what to do."

"Give the baby to his father," I said after a pause. I wasn't sure how she would take this, but it was best for all of us. "I will raise the baby girl as my own, but her brother is at risk staying here. You know this."

I rubbed her arm as she started to sob. Her tears drenched the baby's blanket.

"Baby Jay isn't going anywhere," said Markus, and I glared at him.

"Then we have to hide her and the babies forever," I said. "Is that the type of life Lana wants to live?"

"Why don't you let Alana decide?" said Owen.

Her grandma was silently watching us. Alana sniffled and looked at me with fire in her eyes.

"I'm not leaving my babies anywhere," she said, my worst fears coming true. "I would rather leave Howl's Edge than abandon my child. Not in a million years will that happen. We can wait a couple of months until the babies are older, and then we can leave."

I exhaled loudly, watching the baby girl detach her lips from her mother's breast, content and satisfied as she slept.

"Fine, alright," I conceded. If I wanted to keep her happy, and this was the only way, then I was willing to do this for her. Leaving my family would be tough but I would visit them often.

"Where would we go?" asked Owen.

"Vanessa's husband, Jack has a place out in the human lands," said Grandmother Bianca. "We can check with them if you want to stay there for a little while until you can get more established."

"In the human lands," I said out loud. "How do you feel about that, Lana?"

"It sounds perfect," she sighed, placing the baby girl in my arms so she could rest. My heart swelled as I looked her in the face.

"The boy's name is Jay, huh?" I said. "The girl will be little June."

"Ooh," cooed Alana, her face breaking into the first smile after giving birth. "I love it. You haven't held Jay yet."

My heart started to beat faster.

I wasn't sure if I was ready, but he was my son now. I gently placed June into Owen's arms, who immediately started kissing her face in small pecks.

"Careful, you might wake her," I said.

"Babies never wake up," he said, enamored by her cuteness.

Jay was then placed in my arms. He was sleeping, and his breathing was neutral.

"Does he drink milk?" I asked curiously.

"Yes," said Alana, closing her eyes as she laid back on the pillow.

I stared at the baby's face, and the fear of him trying to kill me when he got older dissipated. The more I held him, the more I didn't want to let go. The weight of him in my arms formed an instant attachment, and I was shocked by my feelings.

"I'll leave you all alone for a few," said Grandmother Bianca, leaving out the door.

171

"Baby Jay," I said out loud. I touched the side of his face, and his small lips curled into a smile.

Tears pricked my eyes.

I would protect my little family at all costs, even if it means moving out of Howl's Edge. I wasn't going to let him go. Anything could happen to him, and it wasn't going to happen on my watch. He would be staked to death if he stayed on Howl's Edge.

"Isn't he adorable?" said Markus, watching me staring into the baby's face. It was out of place to hear a big alpha emanate those words.

"He is," I said, disgruntled that I already loved this baby. "Once the shock of everything was over, I could process things more clearly."

"Don't get me wrong, I was shocked too," whispered Markus since Alana was snoring softly. "But she's still our omega, and she loves us."

"Just as much as that vampire boyfriend of hers?" I said.

Markus snarled at the mention of him.

"She loves us. If she didn't, she wouldn't have trusted us with her huge secret. She knows we're her fated pack."

Chapter 24

Alana

The next morning, Owen was helping me get ready before my family arrived to see the babies. They still had no idea I had given birth, and it was supposed to remain a secret, but Lio had convinced me that they wouldn't tell anyone.

Grandma was cooking lunch downstairs, and Markus was walking around with baby Jay while Lio took care of June. They looked exhausted from the lack of sleep last night, but it felt like a real pack now that the babies were here. For some reason, it felt more lively in the house.

I loved it, but I still felt like something was missing. The actual father of these babies was missing.

"There, your hair is perfect," said Owen, who helped me tie it up in a ponytail.

"Do you see my blue maternity dress over there? Could you get that for me?"

"Alana, they don't expect you to look perfect. You just gave birth, for goodness sakes," said Owen, resting his hand on my shoulder.

"I know, but I can't be naked," I said, looking down at my bare chest. "It's already a lot that my Grandma has seen these jugs."

Owen chuckled and kissed me on the lips, cupping my left breast. I quickly swatted his warm hand away.

"Your grandma is cooking," he said with a twinkle in his eye.

"It doesn't matter. I'm not taking any chances," I whispered, and he kissed me one more time on the lips before grabbing my dress. He helped me put it on, and I grabbed his hand as he led me to the bathroom. I closed the door behind me and used the counter to balance myself as I walked to the toilet. Everything ached, especially my vagina. I couldn't believe I had given birth to twins. It still seemed unreal to me, but I was so excited for my family to see the babies, although I was apprehensive about them meeting Jay. It would be tough for them to understand, and I hoped I wouldn't have to go into detail about the babies.

But they would have to know that I would be leaving Howl's Edge.

Later that day, I heard the doorbell ring.

My heart raced as I looked at the babies lying beside me on the bed. The bed was decorated with a pink comforter from my insistence, and the floor was vacuumed. I was nervous when I heard Grandma greeting my family downstairs. I could hear their voices downstairs, especially my sisters' which were the loudest.

"We have something to show you," said Grandma, leading them up the steps while my dad Grant made a joke in his booming voice.

I looked over at Markus, who was standing next to the bed, and he winked at me.

My heart pounded fast.

"We got this little omega," Markus said. "I can smell your scent changing. You're nervous."

"I don't know what they'll think," I whispered quickly while Grandma glided into the room excitedly.

Grant and my mother walked into the room first, following Grandma. Their eyes widened upon seeing the two bundles on the bed. Mom walked over to me with wonder in her eyes and framed my face with the palms of her hands.

"You had babies," she exclaimed. "Congratulations, daughter! And twins."

"Yeah," I said, smiling, hearing my sisters squealing over the babies.

"Hold on, something is wrong," said Grant, staring at my baby boy in particular. "Something is off about his skin. Very thin and clear."

My mother released my face to see what was wrong. I swallowed hard. Lio's hand rubbed my back comfortingly.

"I have something to tell you," I said.

My entire family looked at me with full attention while I told them the story about the vampire. Some of them looked confused. My sisters didn't care if the baby was a vampire, and they still loved him. Grant was the most pissed off.

"I don't know how I feel about this," he said in a low voice. "You're life is in grave danger."

"I know Dad," I said. "But there's nothing I can do except leave Howl's Edge."

"Leave?!" he boomed. "That should not happen."

"I'm not risking living here."

"Maybe the rules have changed," said Grant.

"Grant, you know better than anyone how much they despise vampires," said Sam. "Our daughter is in danger of being here. Even if you got rid of the baby, and they found out, she would be punished."

Grant's lips thinned in silent anger.

"You should have known better than to go to the beach alone," said Grant.

"Grant," said my mother, laying a hand on his arm. "Please reign in your temper. She had the babies already."

"I'm not happy with any of this. And with her leaving Howl's Edge," said Grant.

Just then, Lio's mother, Keera, walked in carrying a large bouquet. My parents had quieted down about their differing opinions, and the room was now filled with chatter, laughter, and cuddling the babies. My brother Adam was in awe of Baby Jay, watching him like he was some outlandish creature.

"We have an actual baby vampire in this house," said Adam. *"Damn."*

"Adam, don't swear," said Mom sharply, and I smiled. I was content watching everyone having a great time catching up and holding the babies. Soon Grandma announced it was lunchtime, and everyone left the room, including the babies, since my sisters were obsessed with them.

"I'll bring you food," said Lio, and I nodded.

Once I was alone in the room, I was able to take a few deep breaths and relax for a bit. After being in isolation my entire pregnancy, it was draining having to talk to so many people, even if they were my family.

It upset me that Grant wasn't proud of me, but there was nothing I could do about it. I wanted to do great things and impress my family, but my life had taken a different turn than what they wanted.

A turn I had never expected.

I had to use the bathroom. I stood up from the bed and felt instantly dizzy. I grabbed the headboard until I steadied myself. It was torture feeling so weak and tired all the time. As I took tiny steps to the bathroom, my back ached sharply. I paused in the middle of the room, unable to walk further with tears in my eyes. I was in too much pain to walk.

"Baby, what happened?" asked Lio, rushing into the room and setting my plate of food down on the nightstand. He grabbed me by the arm, and I was able to lean on him, relieving the pain in my back.

"I just needed to use the bathroom," I groaned as he walked me to it.

"You should have waited for me," he said, and I heard the panic in his voice. "We shouldn't have left your side."

"It's okay," I said.

"No, it's not okay."

After I used the bathroom, he was waiting outside the door for me. I could still hear everyone downstairs being loud and rambunctious, with Owen being the center of attention. I hooked my arm around Lio's.

"Lana," he said.

"Yes?"

"I'm so sorry about last night. It should have been an exciting moment for us, and you warned me that the baby might not be ours," he said.

"I'm glad you remember it," I said dryly. "I accept your apology."

"I love you. You know that, right?" he said.

"I do," I said, wondering where all this was coming from. *Was it because I said I loved James?* "I hope you're not saying that just because I have a child now, and you're forced to take care of us."

"Listen," said Lio, eyes narrowing. "No one forces me to do *anything*. I want to be here for you and to be the pack of your dreams."

I sat down on the edge of the bed, overwhelmed by what he was saying.

"Are you sure?"

"I've never been so sure of anyone in my life," he said, staring into my eyes. It was so intense, and I felt his alpha energy flow to my soul just from his gaze alone. He meant what he said. "I've always loved you, Lana."

He grasped me by the face and kissed me square on the lips. My heart raced with each brush of his face against mine, his tongue pressing into my mouth. My scent rose as he caressed my hips and my back despite my weak body. He was gentle, and his touch was comforting instead of lustful.

"I want to tell you something," I said. I wanted to tell him that I had to see James before we left and to let him know that he had babies. It would be so wrong to just up and leave. My heart raced.

"Yes?" said Lio.

"Umm, never mind," I said upon second thought. Telling Lio would just start a huge fight. "What food did you get me?"

"All of your favorites."

Chapter 25

***

Two Months Later

Alana

My heart was heavy as I packed my things into a suitcase. Leaving Howl's Edge and my family felt like a nightmare - something I never envisioned doing. Grandma had comforted me numerous times that she would take care of my shop and that I would get used to living in Tennessee. The babies were sleeping in their cribs, and Owen was helping me pack up. Markus and Lio were shopping for supplies that we would need for the trip.

It had taken a while for Grant to come around when he saw no other option except for us to leave, so he agreed to take us with his new helicopter. But there was one thing I needed to do before traveling. I had to see James one more time.

"Owen," I said.

"Mhm?" he said, folding his shirts into a huge pile on the carpet while he sat cross-legged on the ground.

"I'm going to the beach today. I need fresh air," I said. "Being cooped up for two months in hiding is making me depressed."

That part was true.

I had been crying a lot lately, and I knew it had to do with the fact that I needed to see James again. My heart longed to see his kind eyes again, to see him one more time before leaving forever.

"I don't know about that," said Owen. "What if the twins wake up, and I can't handle them both? There needs to be two of us here at all times."

"They won't," I reassured him, pulling the curtain closed to block the sunlight from going on their faces. They were sensitive to bright light. I watched them sleeping in the crib with their hands entwined, and I smiled. "Besides, I'll be back in just an hour. I promise."

Owen walked over to me and wrapped his arm around my waist. His growing black beard brushed my neck as he kissed me, and warmth flooded between my legs. We hadn't been intimate since the babies were born. I hadn't been intimate with any of the men yet until I got stronger. For them to practice abstinence after quitting their knotting jobs took a lot of patience, but I think it helped.

"Do I get a kiss on the lips before you abandon me?"

"Of course," I said with a smile, going on my tip-toes to kiss him. He always smelled the best from the pack with his expensive cologne and frequent showers.

"Don't get into trouble on the beach and come back pregnant," he joked, looking at me like he knew what was going on. I shook my head, not making eye contact in case he could see the lie in my eyes.

"Of course not. That's your job," I joked.

"Yes, you're very right. It's our job to make you pregnant," he said with a dark look in his eyes, and my heart pounded fast.

He reluctantly released me, and I went to my mirror to touch up.

I straightened my black shimmering sweater over my jeans and spritzed some perfume. I had freshly coated pink nail polish today, which made me feel feminine and pretty after a long time of chaos and pregnancy. I was scared and nervous about looking for James today. *What if he had left Howl's Edge? Or if he never wanted to see me again?*

As I walked to the spot on the beach where I had been attacked, my heart was pounding out of my chest, and several times I was getting cold feet, ready to turn back. But I pressed on walking to the spot between the boulders and the hidden cave. In all honesty, I didn't expect to see James and probably never will. I felt like I betrayed Lio, Markus, and Owen by doing this. It was wrong, but James had to know about his babies before we left, or I'd never forgive myself.

But I didn't know how I'd react if I saw him.

I stopped at the rock before entering the secret entrance.

"James?" I called out a couple of times. I couldn't raise my voice in case other vampires heard me. They wouldn't be too happy if they saw me.

After a minute, I gave up and started to walk back toward my car,

"Alana," said a soft voice.

I spun around, seeing him standing at the entrance of the cave. His loincloth was torn in several places as he leaned to the side, his body lanky and muscular. My pulse raced at seeing him again. His familiar face was shaped perfectly, and his striking red eyes made me feel like prey when he gazed at me.

"James," I said in a low voice. He walked over to me, staying careful to remain hidden under the bed of rocks.

"What are you doing here?" he asked, gazing at me like he couldn't believe I was there.

I could tell he was breathing hard, affected by my presence. I couldn't believe I was seeing him again too. I noticed scars all over his arms, and my eyes roamed his body- noticing his body had welts and bruises.

"Oh my god, what happened to you?" I said, rushing over to him and walking around him to inspect. His back was covered in old scars and healing wounds like he had been whipped.

"I took my punishment for helping you," he shrugged like it was no big deal at all.

"No, oh no," I cried, holding my hand to my mouth in horror. It looked so painful, and I felt sick to my stomach that he had to take all that punishment because of me. "I'm sorry, James."

"Hey, it's okay," he said, grasping my forearm.

His touch sent shockwaves through my body, reminding me of what we once had. We locked eyes for a moment, my heart pounding fast. Then I pulled my arm away, which he released instantly.

It was awkwardly quiet for a moment as we gazed into each other's eyes, not sure what to say.

"How have you been?" I asked, breaking the silence. I swallowed nervously because my throat was dry.

"Here and there," he said vaguely. "Volgriff is still pissed off, but I'm helping out with odd jobs for him. Like making sure his betas are alive and fed before the massive feedings, he does with his followers. I'd rather put them out of their misery, but it is what it is."

"Oh, not fun," I said. I opened my mouth to say something about his babies, but I closed my mouth again. I couldn't do it. I couldn't bring myself to tell him. His eyes roamed to my lips, and he took a step towards me. I quickly placed a hand on his chest, stopping him. "We can't."

"It won't get me in trouble," he said gruffly, grasping my hand. Then his eyes widened with realization. "Are you mated?"

I nodded silently.

"Are they treating you well?"

"Yes," I said.

He released my hand and nodded with a serious look in his eyes.

"Then it's time we say goodbye to each other," he said. "Thank you for coming by to see me."

"Yes, of course," I said, and he turned away from me. I turned away, too, slowly heading back to my car with tears flowing down my face. My heart hurt, and my tears wouldn't stop.

I felt for James like I've never felt for anyone before.

Then I felt his cold hand grab mine, and I turned back to face him, wiping my tears with my oversized black sweater.

"I didn't mean to make you cry," he said softly, gazing at my face. I swallowed. "I still think of you, Alana. Every moment of every day. I think of you when I wake up and go to sleep at night. Don't think for a second that I don't care."

His confession overwhelmed me, but it was happening to me too. I wondered how it was possible that he could be my fated mate like Lio. It couldn't be. It could not work even if we wanted it to happen.

"I...you have twin babies," I said, sniffling.

"What?" he asked, unable to hear me over the waves.

"I gave birth a couple of months ago," I said. "To your babies."

"That's impossible," he breathed. He stood frozen in his spot as he stared at me.

"It's true," I said.

"Show me," he said, ready to run out in the streets in what he was wearing. He would stand out like a sore thumb, especially in the area I lived in with Lio and his pack.

"I just wanted you to know before I left Howl's Edge," I said.

"I need to see them," he insisted.

"But look at what you're wearing," I said. "They'll stake you on sight."

"Can you find me something to wear then?" he said, his eyes desolate. "If I can't have you, let me see my children before you leave. I don't have anyone in my life right now."

Especially after what he did to save me. And I knew he was downplaying what happened, but it pained my soul to see him so hurt like this. Physically and mentally, they've worn him down. And the confession of his feelings didn't make my decision any easier.

"Alright," I said. "I'll try to find something, but they'll be awake soon."

Just then, my phone vibrated in my jeans pocket, and I pulled it out, seeing a text from Owen that the babies were awake.

"Shit, the babies are awake."

"That'll be perfect then," said James.

We stood at the front of the house.

James was wearing a large black hat that flopped over his eyes, a pair of pants, and a shirt that I had bought on the way to the house. I could feel the excitement radiate off his body as we stood at the door. I checked to make sure Lio and Markus weren't home before getting out of the car.

"Are you ready?" I asked him.

"More than ready," he said.

I unlocked the door, and I could hear the babies cooing upstairs with Owen singing to them in his deep voice. I smiled, loving that he enjoyed every minute of being with them.

"Stay here," I said to him as I rushed up the stairs. I went inside the room and saw that Owen had the babies on the floor doing tummy time for their crawling exercises.

"Look at June," he said proudly.

"Owen, I have someone here to see them," I said quickly.

"What?"

"It's the father of these children. He wants to see them quick," I said.

"No, the hell he does not," argued Owen in a low voice. "Why the fuck did you bring a vampire to this house? We are *all* going to be thrown in prison or killed."

Chapter 26

James

It blew my mind that she was pregnant the day I left her at the heat clinic. In my heart, I knew I shouldn't have left her.

She was mine even before she stepped foot into the heat clinic.

I had already gone up the steps before Alana could call me inside the room. I knew she wanted to warn whoever was in the room. I couldn't believe I had babies. A family at long last. A family that I couldn't have.

As I stood outside the door, I could hear the harsh whisperings inside as they discussed me. I couldn't wait any longer, and I twisted the doorknob open. The beta looked at me in shock as I strode inside, my focus on the babies. Alana picked up one of them from the floor, and the baby clutched her arms when he saw me. He had on blue overalls, and he peeked over her shoulder to look at me.

My jaw dropped.

His eyes looked like mine, and his black hair. He was a mini-version of myself.

"Alana, this is crazy," muttered the beta, who was clutching the second baby to his chest as he stood trembling on the far side of the room across from me.

"And who are you?" I asked him, annoyed that he was able to spend so much time with the babies while this was my very last and first time seeing them.

"Oh my god," said the beta, unable to speak, staring at me like I was some wild animal.

"This is Jay," said Alana, placing the baby in my arms. I held him upwards to my chest, and he looked at me curiously without crying. My heart felt full and at peace, as I held him while we stared at one another. He would grow up to protect his mother with his soul.

"Hey, little buddy," I said, trying to keep it together. Tears threatened to fall, but I took a few deep breaths. This was my only chance to see them. "My son."

As if he understood, he placed his head between my neck and my shoulder, his chin resting atop my shoulder.

"He loves you already," said Alana.

"Why are you leaving Howl's Edge?" I asked, my protectiveness kicking in now. I didn't realize I had that inside me until I held him. "Why can't you live with me?"

"She's mated to a pack, in case you forgot," said the beta. "Plus, you'll just suck her blood and kill us all."

I ignored him, keeping my focus on Alana. I couldn't let him rile me up.

She and the babies were the only ones who mattered to me. Her soft beauty called to me even though I couldn't have her. My sleepless nights thinking about her was the only thing that soothed me. Or when I took my punishment, all I imagined was her pretty face and the curve of her lips and that I had to go through it to save her.

"He only drinks animal blood," Alana admonished the beta. "Meet your baby girl June before my alphas get home."

"Sure, risk the baby's life," said the beta sarcastically.

My hackles rose at his words. "I would never hurt *my* child. *My* babies, just in case you forgot."

"What the fuck?" said the beta. "While you were the absentee father, I took care of them. They're mine."

I gently handed Alana the baby boy. I would've punched his brains out by now if he wasn't holding my baby girl in his arms.

"Who's this?" said a male voice behind me.

Fuck.

I could tell by the way Alana's eyes widened I knew her alphas had arrived. I turned slowly to face them. One alpha was huge with gray hair and a beard. Next to him was a younger cleanshaven alpha who looked like he had a temper by the way he was glaring at me.

Chapter 27

Alana

All of this wasn't supposed to happen. I shut my eyes tight and reopened them, hoping it was all a bad dream.

Lio was going to kill him. It was in an alpha's nature to protect his family from a threat. And James was the biggest threat of them all.

"Lana, is this the guy?" said Lio, dropping the shopping bags in his hands. Markus followed suit, cracking his knuckles.

"It's nothing," I said quickly, stepping over to James's side. "I invited him here to see his babies before we left Howl's Edge. I thought it would be a good idea."

"That's *not* a good idea," said Lio.

I could feel the tension in the room rising. The alphas and the vampires need to clash and rip each other's heads off. Owen was still staring at James in shock, unable to believe an actual vampire was in the room. James looked very uncomfortable being here, his eyes constantly darting to the door.

"I don't think it's a good idea to disappear without telling me about my children," said James, his eyes trained on Lio. Watching his every

189

move. Lio was also sizing him up as they circled one another. "In fact, Alana shouldn't leave with you at all."

"It's for her safety," said Lio, low growls emanating from his chest. The scent was changing in the room. The scent of war and alpha sweat.

"Lio, it's okay. James was about to leave," I said,

"Oh so, James is his name?"

"Lio, please," I begged. Baby June started to cry, sensing the tension in the room. Owen quickly scooped up baby Jay from me as he ran out of the room with both babies into another room.

"No, this alpha wants to fight. He's a bit immature for you," said James.

"I'll show you what's immature," said Lio swinging a punch at James, and I screamed for them to stop.

But no one was listening. Markus stood there with his arms crossed, watching them wrestle to the ground.

"Fuck you," said James, straddling Lio and punching him square on the jaw. I tried to run in and break the fight, but Markus held me by the arm.

"Let them fight it out," he muttered to me.

"Please, Markus, stop them," I said, trying to pull away from him. He was bulky and muscular, more than capable of breaking up a fight between an alpha werewolf and a vampire. The doorbell rang, and Markus released me. I ran down the stairs to see who was at the door.

It was such a bad time for Grandma to visit.

I needed to tell her to visit another time. Yanking the door open, I gasped when I saw three delta cops with broad shoulders and over seven feet tall.

"Neighbor called because of a commotion happening at this residence," said one of the cops, flashing his badge at me.

"There's no commotion," I said hastily, starting to close the door, but the huge delta wedged his foot between the door and the frame, stopping it from closing.

"We would like to come in and investigate," said the cop.

I could hear the babies crying upstairs, and my stomach flipped with worry. If they ever saw the vampire baby, I would be beside myself.

"There are babies crying," said one of the cops, heading up the stairs.

Before they could climb to the landing, James appeared right in front of them. His red eyes landing from one cop to the other. Then he winked at me. He was risking his life for the babies. I put a hand to my mouth in shock.

"What the actual fuck?" said one of the cops.

"A fucking vampire!" shouted the second one as they ran up the steps. James slid down the railing with his lightning-speed reflexes and waited for the cops to run down the stairs before disappearing out of the door. They chased him out the door, shouting for backup.

I ran to the door, worried about him. Worried if he would make it to safety before they caught him.

I held my stomach, and panic seized me if they caught him. I felt arms encircle me from behind, pulling me back inside.

"What if they catch him?" I said breathlessly.

"He's been hiding all this time," said Lio, leading me to the couch. "He can take care of himself."

"The babies," I gasped. "The police almost saw the babies."

"James made sure they wouldn't," said Lio. "At least he had an ounce of decency left. Especially after raping you."

"He never raped me," I shouted, pulling away from his arms. "I'm tired of you all hating him. He didn't do anything to me."

"I'm sorry," said Lio. "Please don't freak out, Lana. It was a shock seeing him here. Why in the world did you bring him here?"

"I wanted to see...to let him know about his kids," I said, knowing he was still seething. Lio usually needed time to process his emotions before he calmed down.

The rest of the day, I insisted on keeping the television on.

I wanted to see if there was any news about James. No news meant good news, and that was what I was hoping for. But as I was breast-feeding Jay, my head snapped up when the news reporter sounded frantic.

I turned up the volume on the remote, my eyes glued to the screen.

"There's nothing important," said Markus, rubbing my back as he sat next to me.

"Authorities have confirmed the capture of a vampire on Frenshille Road...," the reporter was saying.

"Oh my god," I said, my chest deflating and my stomach turning. "No!"

"He's captured after everything he's done to you," said Markus trying to comfort me. Baby Jay popped his lips off my nipple, and I handed Markus the baby.

"I need a moment," I said, trying to breathe evenly. I could feel the panic creeping through me. Lio ran to the living room, hearing the commotion.

"What's wrong?" he asked me.

"They captured him. They took James," I said, gasping for air and leaning against the couch. "Wait, the Royal Pack is on TV now..."

"Of course, we'll stake him at noon tomorrow, just as tradition states. This has not changed for a hundred years," said King Armon. He was the only living king left, residing in the palace alone with his wife, Queen Ophelia.

"Do you think it might be a little archaic to be doing that?" asked the reporter.

"Chaos will reign if we allow him to live. Nothing will change," replied King Armon.

I paced around the living room in a panic, my hand to my chest. They were going to stake him at noon tomorrow. I had to be there to see him once last time.

"Lana."

"Yes, Lio?"

"Do you still have feelings for the vampire? For James?"

He had finally asked me the question outright. My heart ached at the mention of James. I looked straight into Lio's eyes and nodded.

"Yes. Yes, I do," I said. "Just like I have feelings for you, Markus, and Owen. He's no different."

"Do you trust him with your life?" asked Lio, sitting on the edge of the couch as he watched me thoughtfully with a hand to his chin.

"Yes," I said nervously. Lio was unpredictable when it came to our connection. He could feel threatened and lash out, or he might not even care since the vampire was now stowed away where he couldn't get me.

"Then I don't blame you for feeling the way you do," said Lio, standing up and walking over to me. "If circumstances were different, then I wouldn't mind having an addition to the pack."

"Wait, you'd allow a vampire to mate her?" asked Markus incredulously.

"If that is what our omega wanted," said Lio, and I was surprised by his statement. This was completely unlike him. "But he's going to be staked tomorrow at noon. I can take you there to see him one last time, Lana."

Tears sprung to my eyes.

"Thank you, Lio."

I needed to see him one last time. To reassure him that I was there for him no matter what. And that what was happening to him was completely wrong.

"But if anything goes wrong- we are leaving tomorrow," said Lio. "Your father already has the helicopter stocked and loaded with all our boxes. I've bought your scent blockers in bulk which are also stowed on that plane."

I nodded as he silently hugged me.

"I don't think I can bear to see him get staked," I said. "It's barbaric."

"I know, baby," he said, kissing me on the lips. "I'm sorry."

"I want him to see his babies again," I said.

"It would be very dangerous to bring them," said Lio. "Markus and I will be going with you to the staking. Owen can stay with the twins. I'm not risking the babies' lives."

He was right. It would be risky to do that as a mother.

"Alright."

That night I tossed and turned, ready to feed the babies if any one of them woke up. While I fed Jay in the middle of the night, I stared at his little face thinking about his father, who would be unjustly killed tomorrow.

His father was going to die.

I pressed a hand to my mouth to stop myself from sobbing out loud, feeling sorry for the little baby who would never know his father. After putting Jay to sleep, I got up for a glass of water. I couldn't sleep, and my mind was racing way too much. I made my way downstairs and into the kitchen. My heart was heavy as I sipped on the water, unable to shake off the horrible heavy feeling. I knew my feelings would worsen once James was gone from this world.

I pressed a hand to my racing heart, wishing all this would disappear.

Chapter 28

Alana

The entire island was there to watch the execution and staking of James. I felt sick to my stomach as Markus waded through the crowd so I could be at the front. I needed James to see that I was there.

It would give him some sense of comfort.

As we walked through the sweaty mass of people, my eyes were on James. He was shackled by his wrists to two giant stakes on the ground. His face shined with sweat from the sun, and his eyes no longer glowed with mischief. His eyes were downcast as he gazed at his feet, waiting to die.

I noticed with horror that the executioner was sharpening a wooden stake in his hands. King Armon was there wearing festive red robes. He looked much older as he gazed at the proceedings with delight. It had been the most drama that Howl's Edge had seen in years. His daughter, Princess Lyra, was friends with my mother, and he knew our family. I wasn't sure what he would think if he found out I was associating with a vampire. I couldn't risk mine or the babies' lives. They needed me. We rarely visited his palace since we weren't that close, but he was friends with my father, Grant.

Once we reached the front of the crowd, my eyes were fully focused on James, willing him to look up at least for a second.

"I'm sorry, Lana," said Lio. "I wish I could do something to stop this. I really do."

"It's just too horrible to watch," I whispered, and then James looked up. His eyes met mine, and my chest pounded with fear for him. His eyes softened, communicating to me that it would be alright. That he would be okay. I blinked several times, holding back tears as we locked eyes. I didn't care who was watching us. His face look weak and tired from all his ordeal and sufferings, which would be put to an end today.

"It's noon," said Markus, and my attention shifted to the executioner holding the stake. James also looked at him, and my stomach roiled. I was going to feel sick.

"It is time, my people," said King Armon, who stood before the crowd and held his arms out. I could hear people whispering about the vampire and unable to believe what they were seeing as they stared at him like a spectacle.

My pulse pounded in my head. I watched as the executioner neared James.

I slipped between Lio and Markus, running to stand in front of James. My pulse pounded in my head as I stood under the hot sun on the platform with James behind me. My arms were outstretched to block the executioner. If no one would stand up to this outrageousness, then I would. By god, I would.

"Stop!" I screamed.

"Move, little girl," said the executioner, leering at me.

"Alana?" said King Armon in shock, his eyebrows raised. "Get down from there right now."

"This is wrong," I said. Then louder to the crowd. "This vampire has a good soul, better than any of you. He saved my life."

Lio and Markus quickly strode to my side, their faces shocked at my boldness.

"Alana," James croaked from behind me. "I'll be okay. Don't do this."

With fire and determination in my heart, I refused to leave his side.

"Move," roared the executioner.

"No!" I screamed, standing my ground. Lio and Markus both crouched into fighting position. Ready to defend and protect me if anyone dared attack.

"Whore!" someone shouted from the crowd. Then they all started to chant that phrase over and over.

I looked around wildly, seeing the crowd go out of control. Then everything happened within seconds. Four alphas charged at Markus and Lio. I screamed, running to James and trying to pull the shackles off to free him.

"Leave him alone!" roared Lio's father, Jatix, from the crowd.

With my hand on the burning manacle, I turned to see Jatix transform into his werewolf form along with his pack, Shawn and Silus. Three fully grown alpha werewolves had jumped to the front of the angry crowd, blocking them from getting to Lio.

I gasped when I saw my dad, Grant, also running through the crowd to get to me. He shifted midair into his werewolf form while the rest of my fathers followed suit. Grant stood directly in front of James and I.

Ten alpha werewolves now against a mob of over one hundred.

"What in tarnation is going on?" shouted King Armon.

But it wasn't over.

I heard a loud whistle and turned to see a league of vampires led by Volgriff, wearing loincloths and carrying metal weaponry, rushing toward us. They were holding axes, knives, and even bows and arrows. Volgriff shouted a war cry, and shivers went down my spine.

An all-out war was about to happen, and I could do nothing to stop it.

"Fuck you!" screamed an alpha from the crowd. "Kill'em."

Shouts and screams erupted as the vampires, the Frostcrown Pack and Lustfur Pack, joined forces against the people of Howl's Edge. Bodies were being hurled everywhere, and blood spilled all over the sand. The vampires dodged the frenzied attacks with uncanny agility, retaliating with lightning-fast strikes. Fangs clashed against claws as both sides unleashed their centuries-old animosity upon each other.

"Get yourself to safety," croaked James. "Leave me be."

"No," I whined, trying to pull the manacle off his wrist, but it was futile. My fingers were burning from the hot metal resting under the sun for hours. Then Volgriff charged up to the platform to where we were.

"Move aside, omega," he commanded me with an axe in his hand. I moved, and he hacked off the manacles restraining James. Chaos still raged behind me, and I could hear howls, barks, and whistles from the island's two most powerful alpha packs.

"No!" shouted the executioner, and in a split second, a wooden stake was sticking out of Volgriff's chest.

The executioner had killed the vampire leader. I gasped as Volgriff

199

dropped to the ground, clutching his chest. I didn't care about Volgriff dying, but I cared about James's feelings.

James roared, and the chains on him clanged loudly as they dropped to the ground. He charged at the executioner, wrapping his fingers around his pudgy throat. The executioner gazed in horror at the vampire in front of him. James ripped his head off in seconds and tossed the bloody head to the ground.

I flinched and turned away from the gruesome scene.

I saw my father Grant in his brown fur and Jatix in white fur fighting back to back at anyone trying to get to their children, Lio and myself. I was scared for Wesley since he wasn't much of a fighter, but Sam had his back, and he was a powerful machine gnashing his teeth at anyone who tried to come near.

The crowd was too much for them, though, and even for the king, who was rushing around trying to restore peace. He was surrounded by huge delta guards for safety. It was only a matter of time before all of the vampires were crushed.

Running over to James, I stopped in my tracks when I saw him having a last moment with Volgriff as he lay dying. James was kneeling at the side of Volgriff's body, and I watched as Volgriff handed James his stone necklace with the pendant of a fang.

I hesitantly walked over to James and placed my hand on his bare shoulder. James's wrists were bloody as he stood up and encased my face with his hands. The look of grief on his face was visible. In the midst of the turmoil, our eyes locked. Time seemed to slow as our gazes held, and for a brief moment, the world ceased to exist around us.

"If we die, I need to do this. One last time," growled James.

Then he kissed me in the middle of the battle. His lips brushed against mine, gentle yet demanding, and my heart skipped a beat. His tears and my tears combined as he kissed me with his entire soul. I could feel it in his lips. My eyes closed, absorbing the feeling of his rough hands encasing my face. Protecting me from the world. Our lips meshed as one as we cried together, holding each other.

When we pulled away, there was silence. Utter silence.

I looked at the crowd, at the alphas and the vampires, and saw that they were all watching us. They had all watched us kiss. A kiss that stunned everyone. King Armon looked baffled as he walked up to us. James's eyes narrowed into slits as he pushed me behind him, standing in front of me protectively.

"This is unbelievable," said King Armon.

"Kill her too!" shouted someone, but Armon raised his hand, silencing him.

"Do you love this vampire?" he asked me. I stepped around James despite him clutching my hand in warning.

"I do, until the day I die," I said, my heart pumping fast with everyone watching. "If you kill him, you'll have to kill me too."

"And if you kill her," started Lio as he stood on my other side protectively. He had shifted back into alpha form. "You know the deal."

One by one, all the vampires stood next to James surrounding us. Still in their werewolf forms, Grant and Jatix's pack prowled at the bottom of the platform in front of us.

"We can't keep killing each other," said Armon. Then he looked at James. "You are holding the necklace from your dead leader. Now that you are the new leader, will the feedings stop? Or are you still going to prey on my people?"

James clutched my hand tightly. "It will stop. As the new leader of my people, I will make sure no one feeds on your people in any capacity. I have fed on only animals for years, and I will have my people do the same."

I could see the *Howl's Daily* news reporters getting closer, taking videos and pictures of us. We stood there while King Armon drew up a contract with his advisor, and I watched as James signed the contract in his blood.

"From this day forward, the vampires will live in peace amongst the people of Howl's Edge," announced Armon. "No one is to start a war with one another, and we will have to learn to coexist and live in peace."

Relief coursed through me while he spoke. News reporters harassed the king with questions, and the crowd burst into conversation as they stared at the vampires in fear and disgust. They would need to get used to it. I know I did. And I ended up in love with one of them.

I turned to James, smiling, and he was also smiling through his exhaustion.

"I love you," he said to me, his eyes searching my face.

"I was going to say it first," I whined, and he chuckled, pulling me in for another kiss right in front of Lio. After the kiss, I pulled away and turned to Lio next. "I love you too, Lio."

"Don't forget you're mine too," he grunted, also kissing me hard on the lips. I felt Markus's hands roam on my back, and I turned, kissing him last to the wolf whistles and jeers of the people.

I had freely announced my love with my kisses. And I didn't care who saw as long we didn't get killed for it.

Chapter 29

James

Volgriff's body was heavy in my arms as I walked to my people's village for the burial.

My heart was heavy, and I couldn't look at his lifeless face. The funeral tonight was going to take a hard toll on me. Alana walked beside me along with her two alphas. The vampires who had come to my rescue walked in front and behind us for protection, holding bows and arrows. I was shocked that Volgriff had come out of hiding to save me, but I knew he was looking for any excuse for revenge against the government. I thought he despised me for what I had done. There was a love-hate relationship between us. He took care of me like a father would after my family was killed.

"Are we going back to your village?" Alana asked me, looking up at me with her beautiful wide eyes. Her long eyelashes fluttered as she gazed at me with concern.

"I would prefer you stay in the safety of your city," I grunted. Sweat trickled down the back of my neck from the long walk to the cave. We were getting nearer, and I was worried about what my people would say once they saw her.

"No, I'm coming with you," she said, looking straight ahead. "Please don't tell me to leave you again."

Her alpha glanced at me with disapproval in his eyes, but at least it wasn't in ultimate hate this time.

"Are you the leader of the pack? I'm not sure how all this works," I asked him.

"Yes, my name's Lio," he said, introducing himself and about to shake my hand but held back when his eyes landed on the dead body in my arms. "I'm sorry for your loss."

"He was like a father to me," I said gruffly. I was wary about divulging too much information with an alpha who shared my omega's heart.

"Oh hell, that's tough," said Lio, shaking his head as he looked straight ahead. "I can't even imagine."

I nodded, not saying anything else. I didn't trust myself speaking in case I broke down, showing weakness in front of her alphas.

"It's odd she's in love with you too," said the second alpha, who looked much older than Lio. "I'm Markus, by the way. Pleased to make your acquaintance in battle."

"Markus, he just lost somebody close to him," said Alana, who gripping his hand.

"Sorry man," said Markus, glancing at Volgriff's body.

"It's fine," I said shortly, and the alphas finally stopped trying to make conversation with me. I wasn't in the mood right now. "You all don't need to come with me to the funeral."

"Wherever Alana goes, we go," said Lio. "Without question."

"Sounds dandy," I said, and Alana glanced up at me with pain in her eyes. I knew she wished I could get along with her alphas, but it just wasn't happening right now. I wanted her with my entire soul, and sharing her love with alphas sickened me.

When we reached my secluded community between the mountains, the vampires waiting for their warriors watched us in silence. They were staring at the werewolves walking in with me and at their dead leader in my arms.

Volgriff's aunt, Fran, and Volgriff's brother rushed to me with horror etched onto their faces.

"What happened?!" screamed Fran, clutching her white hair.

"He died during battle," I explained. The brother silently took him from my arms. The vampires assembled before me, staring at the alphas and the omega.

"What is *she* doing here?" said the brother snidely, giving Alana a dirty look. I stood in front of Alana, blocking her from everyone's gaze.

"We are not to touch her or her alphas. The government had agreed to allow us to live in peace amongst them," I said, and the brother spit on the sand.

"Fuck no," he said. "We will stay here until the day we die. There's no fucking way we'll live under their mercy."

They had just dealt with a severe loss, and I needed to be patient.

Volgriff's brother took the body from my arms before the funeral. They were grieving, and rightly so. The other vampires stood there expectantly, looking at the stone necklace on my neck and waiting for me to command.

To lead them.

"Volgriff gave me this necklace before he passed," I said.

They somberly bowed their heads at the mention of their beloved leader. The one who couldn't do anything wrong, even though I disagreed with him so many times.

"What are you going to do now?" asked a young vampire in his teens.

"You all need to start with mind-wiping all the captured betas and setting them free."

Alana

It was scary how many betas they had captured into cages.

I watched as each beta stumbled out of the vampire encampment one by one, looking confused after being mind-wiped by the vampires at the cage entrance. I found a large boulder to sit on while Markus paced around in front of me. I knew this wasn't easy for James as I watched him barking out orders to the vampires. They were hesitant to obey him at first since he took away their main meals, but the necklace he was wearing seemed to hold much significance to them, so they had to respect him.

The funeral was a somber event as we stood off to the side watching when they placed a large black cloth over Volgriff's house. His body was wrapped in white cloth and set on a pedestal. Three elderly vampires surrounded the body, anointing his face with droplets of oil.

As I watched the proceedings, I thought about my relationship with James. I didn't want it to be over just because he was the leader now of his people now. I knew it was irrational to be together, but my heart wouldn't let me think otherwise.

Later that night, as I hung out with Markus- I saw Lio and James talking in the distance.

"What are they talking about?" I said out loud.

"No idea," said Markus, with his hand on the small of my back. "But I'm getting tired as fuck. We should be going home soon."

But without James? I thought silently.

My heart pounded faster as Lio and James approached us in the night.

"We've come to an agreement," said Lio.

"Umm, what kind of an agreement?" I asked, confused.

"I can tell you're very much in love with James," said Lio. "And you're much happier than I've seen in months."

"How do you know I'm happier?" I asked. I had gone through several heartbreaking nightmares of James gone. Months of depression had taken hold of me, but I'd try to smile and act like everything was alright.

"I can tell, babe," said Lio.

"I will divide my time between you and coming here to lead my people," said James. "Once things start to settle down, I'll visit you often. And every day during your heats. How does that sound?"

"But...tonight, will you stay with us?" I asked. I knew it was huge and probably selfish of me since he had just lost his leader, but I wanted to cuddle with him tonight, and I couldn't bear to tear myself away.

"What?" said Markus in shock.

"Just tonight," said James. "I miss the babies and I miss you, Alana."

"I missed you too," I said, my voice high-pitched with emotion. He leaned towards me but stopped.

"If I wasn't covered in blood, I'd hug you right now."

A couple of hours later, Owen stared at all of us wide-eyed when we entered the house past midnight. We were all covered in blood, especially James, and we looked rough as hell as we took off our shoes at the doorway. I felt exhausted to the bone, but all I could think about was hugging James and catching up on missed time.

"What happened?" Owen asked. "The babies are finally sleeping, and I couldn't watch the news."

"James will stay the night with us," I said.

"What?!"

"Just for one night until we can figure something out," I said. Owen looked over at Lio for help, but Lio simply nodded. Not a word passed between them. I started to wonder if I pissed off my pack, but they clearly agreed that this was okay. "Come, James."

I grabbed him by the hand, and we walked upstairs to the largest bathroom in the mansion. I wanted us to shower before we saw the babies.

"Where are you taking me, omega?" he asked.

"To the shower," I said, leading him to the door.

"Aren't you coming in with me?" he asked.

"I thought you might want some space..."

He tugged me by the waist into the bathroom, shutting the door with his foot. "The only space I want is the one between your legs, little omega."

I giggled as we quickly stripped at top speed. I peeled off my blood-stained jeans, shirt, and underwear. He threw his loincloth in the trash.

"Alright, let's get in here," I said, stepping into the glass doors and turning on the shower. I watched James's look of pure pleasure as he stepped in after me, just standing under the water.

"God, I missed a real shower," he groaned, his long black hair plastered to his face as he gazed at me. "This is nice. Very nice."

I slathered soap onto my skin, smiling while he enjoyed himself under the water. But he quickly grabbed my shower rag and started washing me instead.

"Ooh," I said as he circled the pink rag around my breasts.

"Hold on, I haven't kissed you properly yet," he grumbled, moving his face to mine and kissing me hard. He cupped me between my legs with the rag as we kissed wildly under the water. I missed him so much, but at the back of my mind, I was worried about my pack. "There's something on your mind, my love."

"I'm worried Lio might be feeling bad," I said in a low voice while our wet bodies were pressed together in the shower.

"Don't be," he said, his eyes studying my face. "I may not be officially part of the pack, but I am yours, and you are mine. Just as you are to them."

"That makes me feel better," I said, gasping as he pressed a finger between my legs.

"Good," he growled against my lips, and I shivered in his arms. He was all around me, muscular, tall, and powerful. My stomach fluttered as he washed me with his bare hands all over my body. His hands were callused and rough against my skin as he washed my legs. Then he knelt before me and pressed his mouth against my pussy. "Oh, how I missed your tight little pussy."

He gripped my ass cheeks and prodded my legs open with his nose. I willingly obliged. I missed his touch, his calming presence, and his sexual energy. Everything about him made me come alive under his fingertips.

"Is this wide enough for you?" I asked him, spreading my legs further and gripping his wide shoulders so I didn't slip. He licked my pussy in one swoop, and my belly clenched with desire.

"Did you miss my tongue on your pussy?"

"Yes," I breathed, feeling his cold breath on my pussy when he spoke. He licked again, and the cold contrast of his tongue against the warmth of the water was too much. My knees buckled as he continued to lick me in long strokes. His thick tongue pressed into my pussy, jabbing inside me, stretching me open.

"I need your slick babe," he said, voice muffled. His shoulders flexed under my fingers as I moaned. "Delicious."

He released one of my ass cheeks and pushed a finger into my pussy while he licked my clit in faster strokes. I moaned and bucked on his face. He slipped a second finger into my pussy, while furiously sucking my clit. The tension in my belly rose and rose until it finally snapped into a wave of pleasure. I gripped his shoulders as I yelped through my ecstasy. I tried closing my legs and pulling away, but he hadn't had his fill.

"Oh," I moaned, trying to pull away from his grip on my ass cheeks. "I'm done."

"*I'm* not done," he growled, continuing to lick me in softer circles until I was weak in the legs. "One more time, little omega."

He pumped his fingers into me, and I could feel my pussy stretching when he placed a third finger. I groaned in delight, and more slick squeezed from my pussy in his persistence.

"We're supposed to be showering," I moaned as I felt myself coming close. He started to suck on my clit again, and I trembled all over as I rode my second orgasm in a row. "Oh, my moons."

He finally released his grip on my ass cheeks and softly licked my pussy before the shower water washed me clean. Then he lifted me up against the wall of the shower, and I wrapped my legs around his waist.

He lifted me up further until his dick speared into my pussy. My eyes rolled back in pleasure.

"I missed fucking you," he growled in my neck. He started thrusting into me, bouncing me up and down on his dick. It felt so fucking good, I could cry.

"I missed it too," I moaned in his ear. He scratched my neck with his fangs, and I longed for him to bite me. My heart pounded fast, and my pussy squeezed around him.

"Fuck yes," he grunted with each thrust into me. I felt his hunger. His raw masculine need to take what he needed at this moment was enough to turn me on. "I dreamed of taking you like this. Under the water."

"Oh," I squeaked when he jammed his cock deep into my pussy. Deep, slow, powerful strokes while he nipped and kissed my neck.

"You're mine. Say it."

"I'm yours," I whispered.

"Look at me, Alana."

I turned my face to look at him face to face. His eyes glowed red as he plunged one more time inside of me.

"I love you," he roared, and his hips bucked. His semen sprayed into

211

me, filling me like an alpha's would but without the knotting.

And it was okay. Because...

"I love you too, James," I said, kissing him on the lips. He kissed me back while his cock was still deep inside me. Unmoving and unwilling to part from me.

He held me against him, and I hugged him back. We stood like that for a while until I lost track of time- with my head pressed against his collarbone and my legs wrapped around him.

Chapter 30

Alana

The next morning, I swept up the broken pieces of glass from the floor of my shop, and my heart was breaking as I stared at the smashed windows. Grandma was helping me as she swept up the other side of the shop. Last night, after the hottest shower of my life, James watched the babies eagerly while I slept. He refused to sleep and instead wanted to spend time with his babies under Owen's watchful eye. I was reluctant to leave the house, but James had to go back to his people to lead, and Markus took over watching the babies along with Owen insisting it was fine for me to leave. I was singing in my car on my way to the shop, happy that everything was coming together and we would have a nice cozy routine.

But Grandma and I had come to a disaster in the shop.

"This has to be retaliation," I said. "They don't want me to be with a vampire."

"The hate runs deep," said Grandma. "There's nothing you can do until it passes. They will get over it."

"We need to get cameras or something."

213

"I agree."

We kept the shop closed as we cleaned and straightened the shelves. We lost so much merchandise. It was terrible. I would have to get new windows and take from the budget. When the door opened with the sound of the jingle, I jumped thinking it was one of the thugs who broke in.

But it was only Lio, and I was relieved to see him.

"I noticed the broken windows from outside," said Lio, walking in and looking around. He came over to me, touching my elbow, and I stopped sweeping the floors.

"There are damn criminals running around here," said my grandma, who was pissed off all day. I could tell she was pissed off by how her glasses hung above her head and how her hands shook more than usual today. "Just because my granddaughter fell in love with a vampire."

"It's unacceptable," said Lio with a hard line to his jaw. "I will install cameras all over the store, and we will replace your windows."

"No, it's okay. It's not in the budget," I said.

"Not in *your* budget," he said. "I'm paying for the repairs."

"Lio, I can't accept it," I said, my eyes burning as I stared at the shelf. "It's my fault this happened."

He turned my face to look at him. "It's not your fault baby. You were destined to be with him, and that's all there is to it."

My chin wobbled with emotion, as he kissed me.

"Thank you," I whispered.

"Anything for you, my love."

One Month Later

"Do you have any more of the keychains shaped like a fang?" asked a customer.

"I'm sorry, I've run out of those," I said, and her face fell. My vampire merchandise was a top seller, and I couldn't keep up with the demand. James had his people carve out the little wooden trinkets, and I paid them a portion of the earnings.

"We have more," said James, walking into the shop with a box in his hand and wearing a fancy black suit with a white dress shirt and black tie.

"Yay!" said the customer, running to the counter.

I smiled as he set the box down on the counter, and the ten customers flocked to purchase them with the help of my grandma. Things had improved with the people being more accepting of the vampires as they integrated their lives on Howl's Edge. The vampires kept to themselves mostly, even though the females were fascinated by them. A customer even asked if the vampire sucked on my blood while an alpha knotted me. I was shocked by the question, but it was also playing in my mind, and I would get aroused thinking about it.

"Little omega," said James, approaching me. His hands rested on my waist, and I pulled him to the back of the shop for some privacy. I closed the door to the backroom, and he trapped me in his arms.

"Why are you dressed up in a suit?" I asked, touching his neatly shaven face. His black hair was tied back in a bun, without a stray hair in place, and he smelled like woody cologne. He brought his lips to my neck, kissing me there. Lio, Markus, and Owen also had their intimate favorite spot on my body, which I loved.

"I came to whisk you away somewhere," he muttered, his cold

breath causing goosebumps to form on the back of my neck and butterflies in my belly.

"But I'm working," I said. "We need to help Grandma."

"We're closing shop right now, then," he said.

"How will I make money?"

"I'm sure you can squeeze a penny or two from Lio," he said, and I giggled. I loved having my own source of income even though they all wanted to take care of me, buy me things, and spoil me.

"Don't you have a vampire land to run?" I asked him.

"It's different now that some of them have moved into the city."

"Are you worried they'll start feeding on people?"

"No, they love the luxury life a little too much," said James. "Although I get worried about seeing a dead beta on the news. No mark on the neck means good news. So far, they're being careful."

"That's good," I said as he kissed me on the neck. He groaned, pushing me up against the wall as his cool lips pressed onto my skin. I longed for his fangs to sink into me and suck my blood again. "You can drink a little bit."

He groaned again, pulling back from me.

"Don't tempt me," he said. I knew he was scared of losing control. It made me sad each time he turned me down and Owen thought I was nuts for wanting it but I didn't care.

Later that day, James waited in the car while I got ready in the house. I walked to the bedroom and gasped when I saw a beautiful flowing red dress with lace sleeves lying on the bed with a note on top of it.

Wear this tonight, love- Lio

Excited, I quickly ran into the shower, washing up at top speed and shaving every part of my body.

I hadn't had a date ever since the babies were born. My mother, Tiana, was watching the babies today, to the delight of my sisters. I was already missing June and Jay since my normal routine after work was to hug and kiss them. After I slathered on a nice-smelling lotion, I pulled the dress on, carefully tying the gold sash into a bow behind me. It fit like a glove, the lace sleeves overflowing past my arms like a butterfly. The sparkle and jewels on the dress looked stunning as I admired it in the mirror.

Then I blow-dried my hair until it cascaded in waves down my shoulders and my back. Today, I went all out with my makeup. I put on a layer of foundation and spent a bit of time doing my eyebrows. Then I put on matching red lipstick to match my dress, a bit of shimmering eyeshadow, and blush.

Being told to wear a certain dress and taken to a secret location sent happy thrills up my spine. I spritzed perfume on myself that complimented my natural scent, and I was ready to head out the door.

James was waiting downstairs for me as I walked down the stairs. He held a bouquet of roses for me, and my heart lifted.

"Aww, you didn't have to," I said.

"Anything for you," he said, handing me the flowers and kissing me gently on the lips. "Are you ready to go, my sweet?"

"Yes," I said, smiling.

In the car, James played soft romantic music on our way there. I stared out at the night sky and the twinkling stars thinking about how James came a long way to be here. He had blended well into the family, loving me in his own quiet way away from the rest of the men.

I wanted to love them all at once in one room, but James was uncomfortable with that. He enjoyed having me to himself every chance he got. He would volunteer to watch the babies a lot so I could have my private time with the alphas. Especially during the times when Markus took me in my pussy and Lio would take my ass in the next room. Owen was the most worried parent, careful about any child entering the room by accident and strict rules around the house to prevent that from happening, making sure the door was locked even though the babies couldn't walk yet.

"We're here," said James, parking the car in front of a garden.

"Oh," I said in awe as I stepped out.

We walked hand in hand into the beautiful garden with beautifully trimmed shrubbery, over the rocks melded together with a stream of water underneath. In front of us was a giant fountain that trickled softly, casting a glow over the three figures standing in front of it.

Lio, Markus, and Owen.

All of them were standing there proudly in their suits, and they had smiles on their faces as they watched me walking across the stone path to them.

I smiled back, feeling sexy in my dress which flowed at my feet. I was uncomfortable from my heels clicking on the stone pathway, and I couldn't wait to rip them off later.

"Hi, my loves," I said softly. They quietly surrounded me, kneeling down on one knee, including James. "Oh my god."

My cheeks burned with embarrassment at all the attention on me at this moment. I never expected this to happen.

"Lana," said Lio, holding out a small red velvet box and snapping it open. I gasped out loud when I saw the ruby-red rock encircled with diamond stones. "I've always loved you. All my choices in life were made because of you. And for years, I came to your shop, wishing you'd look my way, but here we are now, and I have this vampire to thank for. For him bringing you to my doorstep."

It was his own subtle way of making James feel welcome.

James was next as he looked me earnestly in the eye and grasped my hand. My heart was beating so hard I knew they could hear it with their heightened alpha and vampire senses. My scent was thick in the air, and I clenched my thighs together in my nervousness and excitement.

"Thank you Lio," said James. Then he turned to me. "Since the day you crashed into my little village, I knew you were mine. The day I saw your trembling small form in my hut, emotions that had remained dormant for years came alive. I didn't allow myself to feel until you came into my life, and for that, I'm grateful. I pledge to love you, to protect you until the end of my life."

Then he released my hand, and Markus wrapped his large warm paw around my hand, gazing into my teary eyes.

"Alana," he began. "It all started in the heat clinic for me. You've brought my soul back to life. Your scent invigorates me and charges me like no other omega. Fate has meshed us together in this mysterious way, and there's no way I will refuse it. I will protect you with my heart, soul, and body until I die."

Now the tears were flowing down my cheeks.

I couldn't help it.

They were putting their hearts out on the table, releasing all their emotions tonight. Markus released my hand, and I turned to Owen, who grasped my hand in both of his. His voice, tinged with both trepidation and excitement, expressed the depth of his emotions as he spoke.

"Hey, sweetheart," he said smoothly, and I smiled through my tears. "Since the moment you showed up to be our patient, I knew something would change. Your beauty surpasses all others, and your strength and kindness inspire me daily to be better. I may joke a lot, but I'm being serious when I tell you that I love you Alana."

Tears streamed down my face. These men were serious about me, and ready to commit their life to me. He released my hands, and Lio spoke next.

"Lana, will you do me the incredible honor of being our mate? To walk hand in hand with you forever?" Lio asked with a sparkle in his eye. As we looked into each other's eyes, I remembered the boy who was in love with me from the beginning. The boy who I was excited about at the campfire years and years ago.

Overwhelmed by the sincerity and depth of his proposal, my heart soared with joy.

"Yes to all of you," I said, my voice betraying my emotion as it cracked. "I would love to spend the rest of my life with all of you, however different we all are."

Then he slipped the blood-red ring on my finger, the jewels shining brightly from the glow of the fountain.

"She looks so good with that on," said Markus, admiring my finger as I smiled and held it up to them.

"We're engaged!" I squealed as Lio picked me up and spun me around.

Chapter 31

Alana

"Where are we going?" I asked breathlessly as Lio carried me in his arms after spinning me in the air.

"To that hotel," he said gruffly.

"What about the kids?!"

"They'll stay overnight with your mother," answered James, who surprisingly got along with my mom. Grant was still on guard when it came to James, but he said it was entirely my choice if I wanted to be with a vampire.

Lio spanked my ass.

"What was that for?" I squealed.

"For thinking we were being irresponsible with the kids," he said, spanking me hard on the butt again. My cheeks burned, but all it did was arouse me. I tried clenching my thighs together, but his arm was wedged in the middle of my legs, his hand on my lower back. "I can smell you."

"Oh," I whimpered. "Please put me down."

"If you make that request again, I'll spank you again," he growled in my ear, and I hushed right there. My ass cheeks were already burning and sending tingles to my pussy. When we entered the hotel, I marveled at the fancy high ceilings. I was embarrassed that Lio was carrying me as we checked into the hotel. The concierge didn't say anything, as if it was a normal occurrence for an alpha to come in with his omega cradled in his arms and ready to be fucked.

In the hotel room, Lio finally set me down on the bed. The men were quickly removing their shoes, suits, and ties.

"Are you ready for all of us?" asked Lio gruffly, kneeling on the floor between my knees as I sat on the edge of the bed. His question made my cheeks burn bright. I had never been in a room with all of them at once. Usually, one or two of them were babysitting, or James didn't like to be there with everyone. I bit my lip. "Say what's on your mind, Lana."

"I have a fantasy I'd been thinking about," I said.

At my words, all the men surrounded me- listening closely with their ties in disarray and pants half off, exposing hairy thighs.

"What is that fantasy?" asked Markus, ready to fulfill whatever my heart desired. No matter how base it seemed.

"I...I want James to bite my neck while two of you. You know," I whispered shyly. They were all watching me with their glowing eyes, muscular and big. Ready to please me.

"Know what?" asked Lio, daring me to say it. I didn't look up at him, instead focusing on the lace pattern of my sleeve.

"While two of you fuck me," I said, looking up at him finally.

"I might lose control," said James finally after a short silence.

"Oh, it's okay then," I said, biting my lower lip in embarrassment. "I thought we could try something a little crazy."

"But," said James, lifting my chin with his finger. "I've done it before, and I'm ready to taste you again, my sweet."

I clenched my thighs together at his words, shocked at how much that turned me on. I was finally going to feel it again. The memory of him sucking my blood while fucking me in front of all the vampires played through my mind, arousing me even further. It was a high I wanted to feel again.

James

The omega trembled as she stood in the middle of the room while I untied her sash from behind. She looked amazing in her red dress, hugging her full breasts heavy with milk. My cock hardened as I rubbed her back and down the curve of her buttocks over her dress. She looked magnificent and voluptuous. The dip of her back for her large ass was enough to cause precum to leak from me.

Markus and I lifted her dress.

"Arms up, baby," said Markus, and she obeyed, lifting her arms.

Fuck.

Even though she was a tough little omega outside of the bedroom, she was soft, and pliant in bed with her alphas- her submissiveness making me rock hard. She wore the tiniest red thong that did not fit her large butt, and her breasts were dying to be set free, constrained in her black lace bra. My eyes were on her jiggling creamy breasts as Owen unsnapped her bra from behind.

"Look at how magnificent her breasts are," said Markus, cupping one while Lio grabbed the other, squeezing her luscious tits.

I was dying to bite her already. The taste of her blood from the first time had never left me. Her blood was smooth and silky, the only thing that quenched my true thirst. Animal blood wasn't the same at all. It was only enough to keep me alive. But her blood made me stronger, invincible even. Raw strength flowed through my body for a month after I fed on her.

I needed her again. To taste her again.

"Let's go to the bed," I said, my voice hoarse. I smelled her scent filling the air in anticipation of us. She was ready for me to feast on her while her alphas fucked her. I would fuck her right after. She was all mine after they were through with knotting her. There was no mistake about that.

We gently laid her out on the bed as I came around to the head of the bed, near her neck.

"Alright, Lana, it's your choice," said Lio. "Who do you want to take your ass?"

"Owen," she said softly. The rise of pink in her cheeks was unmistakable. "I don't want to be knotted in my backside tonight."

"Who do you want to take your pussy while James feeds on you?"

"You, Lio," she replied. It fucking turned me on when she was acting so innocent. She knew she wanted us to fuck her hard but was too shy to say it.

Then in her ear, I whispered, "it'll be my turn next. I will fuck your pussy after Lio thoroughly knots you."

"Oh, James," she said, breathing hard at my naughty words.

Alana

I wasn't prepared when James placed his cold lips on my neck, whispering about all the dirty things he would do to me. Owen was rubbing my ass cheeks in preparation before he plunged into me and Lio rubbed my thighs while I was lying on my side in the middle of them. Lio was laying in front of me, watching my face as he lifted my leg over his, separating my thighs.

"No time to be shy now," said Lio, rubbing my arms. "You were bold during your heat, but now you're a little shy during group activities again, aren't you?"

"I'm not shy," I protested, but when he lifted his leg, spreading my pussy wider, I started to clench my thighs.

"Hmm, I don't think so," said Lio, bringing his face to mine and kissing me until I was breathless and squirming from arousal all over the bed. Then he dipped his finger between my legs, brushing my clit in soft strokes. Teasing me.

James's cold lips on my neck felt exquisite as he kissed and sucked his way to the spot he wanted to bite. Owen was spreading my ass cheeks apart, and I felt his finger probing around my anus, stretching me. Markus was oiling and massaging my feet while I was surrounded.

"Oh gosh," I said, feeling Lio's finger dip inside my pussy.

James's hand snaked in front of me, between my breasts, and traveled down, rubbing my clit and squeezing it. He played with my clit while Lio pushed his finger deep inside my pussy.

"Get in there Lio," said James. "I've got her clit in my fingers."

"Fuck yes," said Lio, thrusting his finger in my pussy as I squirmed. There was so much sensation going on down there I couldn't handle it, but I didn't want it to stop. Owen's finger pushed in and out of my anus, and warmth flooded my pussy. Slick dripped from both places the more Lio and Owen plunged their fingers in and out.

James's fingers played underneath the hood of my vagina, squeezing and fondling my clit.

"So fucking hot," said Markus, rubbing my feet over his cock as he watched me. "Fuck her with two fingers."

"More than happy to," said Lio, stretching me wide when he plunged his pointer finger inside me. Owen did the same, pushing a second finger into my ass as they pulled and thrust into me at the same time.

"Oh," I moaned. I was so close. My belly clenched with my impending orgasm. With the feeling of all these fingers inside of me and James pinching and rubbing my clit. I put a hand to my mouth to block my scream as my orgasm took over.

"Go ahead and scream baby," said Lio, plunging a third finger inside of me. James pressed my clit hard in circles. Owen pressed another finger inside my ass, pounding into my butt.

I gripped the sheets screaming as I rode the waves. My pussy clenched, and my clit was extra sensitive as I tried to move away from James's fingers. But he gently rubbed my pulsing clit with less force while I tried to come down from my earth-shattering orgasm.

"Oh yes, she's a screamer," said Owen as he kissed the back of my shoulder and removed his fingers from my ass. "I'm going to put my dick inside your little ass. Are you ready? You've been such a good little omega, and you deserve it."

"Yes," I said.

"Spread your ass cheek for me, sweetie."

While Lio buried his cock inside my pussy from the front with my leg wrapped around him- I reached behind me, but Markus's hand stopped me.

"I'll hold you open for Owen's cock to go inside you," said Markus gruffly. Whenever one mate wasn't actively involved in the sex, they were usually there to support and help me, so I didn't have to do anything except enjoy everything they were giving me.

His large warm hand gripped my ass, spreading my cheeks apart.

I felt the tip of Owen's cock pressing inside my anus, spreading me. It was much bigger than his fingers, and I had to brace myself for the thickness of his cock. I clutched Lio's upper arm, his strong muscles flexing underneath my fingers. In seconds, they were thrusting into me. I gasped when I felt James's fangs piercing my skin, his cold lips numbing the pain.

Arousal strummed to my pussy when he sucked my blood and fed on me. My pussy and ass clenched tight when he drew more blood into his mouth while Lio fucked my pussy.

"Oh fuck," said Markus, watching me getting penetrated on both sides. His hand was working his cock as his white liquid spurted all over the hotel floor. James released my neck, and I felt a little dizzy but horny as Lio pounded into me from the front and Owen from behind. His hips would thrust forward each time, taking control and fucking me from the side.

"Your ass is nice and warm, hugging my dick," whispered Owen. "Do you like it when I fuck your ass with my dick that can't knot?"

"I like when you're in my ass," I gasped when he gripped my ass cheek and plunged deeper.

Lio roared as he came, thrusting his cock deep inside my pussy.

His hot liquid streamed into me, and it felt so good. When his cock knotted, I sighed with pleasure, feeling the familiar stretch of my pussy walls that I craved all the time- especially during my heats.

"Ahh, that felt amazing," said Lio, kissing me hard as Owen came next. I felt his dick plunge one last time into my ass, his balls slapping against my cheeks.

"Fuck," said Owen, spilling inside my ass before pulling out. He slowly pulled out and spread my ass cheeks apart to inspect what he'd done. "My cream is all over your little ass. It looks so good on you, baby."

James was licking my neck, ensuring no blood drops spilled down. I enjoyed his tongue on my neck, and the pain from the bite heightened everything about this mating.

"How was your little fantasy?" asked Lio with a wink.

"More than I dreamt of," I sighed happily in his arms. They all surrounded me on all sides, kissing and touching me while I was still knotted to Lio. We laid like that for thirty minutes while I basked in their love and the after-knotting glow.

When Lio's knot deflated, James was immediately on top of me, his cock thick and ready.

"I can't just feed on you and not fuck you," he growled, plunging his dick into my pussy. It sounded like a suction since Lio's liquids were still inside me. My heart pounded with arousal as I wrapped my legs around his waist. James liked to be intimate with me one on one. All to himself. But this time, he was fucking me in front of everyone.

"This feels so good," I sighed before his lips crushed mine. His body was lighter above me and not as heavy as the alphas.

His hips pistoned into me at high speed, ramming his dick into my pussy that had been stretched not long ago from Lio's knot.

James's tongue plundered my mouth, and my tongue found his. We frenchkissed as he continued to ram into me with his dick. I moaned against his lips, not wanting him to stop as his penis hit my sensitive places repeatedly.

He groaned against my mouth in one last thrust when he released inside of me.

"Oh god, I needed that," he groaned again, kissing me hard as his dick twitched inside me, releasing his last few drops. "I love you, Alana."

Then he pulled out, collapsing next to me. I was breathless by the time he rolled off of me. It was the most intense sex I've ever had.

"I love you too," I said.

"We all love you Lana," said Lio with hooded eyes, still lying on his side as he watched James fuck me. "During your next heat, you'll get pregnant with quadruplets."

My horrified expression made Owen laugh out loud.

"The twins are already a handful," I said.

"I can't wait to see her belly round again," said Markus, laying his hand on my stomach and rubbing me. "I'm going to let you rest, little omega. Then I'm going to knot inside you next. I'm going to put a baby in you."

My heart pounded hard at his determined statement. His eyes conveyed how serious he was. He was already such a good father, and I never doubted him.

"I would love to have more babies one day," I whispered, and he looked at me with such adoration my heart melted. "I love you all, and I can't wait to grow our little family so our twins can have some brothers and sisters running around."

"That's right," said Markus, kissing each of my swollen breasts. His tongue shot out licking off some of my milk dripping down my stomach. "Spoken like a true omega."

I lay in contentment between James and Lio, lazily playing with Lio's chest hairs with a smile. Their arms were wrapped protectively around me as we laid there. Lio pressed a kiss to my forehead and whispered, "you were incredible."

And James nuzzled his lips against the crook of my neck, planting soft kisses on my collarbone.

"Absolutely breathtaking," said James, his breath sending shivers down my spine.

Epilogue

One Year Later

Alana

On the morning of my wedding, the sun's golden rays cast into my room while my mother curled my hair.

I sat in my plush pink chair, watching Tiana curl the front tendrils of my hair in concentration, her tongue sticking out as she usually did when she was focused. I was already showered and wearing a white tank top and leggings until Grandma could bring my dress.

The night before, I barely got any sleep, tossing and turning to the annoyance of Lio, who was a light sleeper. I was so excited for today.

A day I had been dreaming about for months.

My babies were getting dressed with the help of my younger sisters. They were downstairs and causing a racket while Jay knocked stuff off the counters, which I didn't have the energy for. I could hear what was going on from the dishes crashing and Roxanne freaking out. June was the quiet twin who loved to dress up like a princess and watched me carefully every time I did my makeup. I couldn't help but laugh every time. Everyone who met her loved her instantly, but Jay, on the other

231

hand, was quite the handful and spoiled rotten by Lio.

My mom and I were in the room with the door closed to minimize some of the noise. A solemn mood came over me all morning, something weighing heavy on my mind recently.

"Mama, I have to tell you something," I said.

"Of course, my dear. You can tell me anything," said Tiana. Her voice was always calm and soothing, dispelling some of my fears. I took a deep breath, my stomach clenching with nervousness.

"When I was seventeen, do you remember the field trip I took with my class?"

"Hmm, there were many field trips," she said, brushing my hair.

"Well, we had a camping one overnight," I said. "And..."

"What is it?" she asked, her voice tinged with worry now. She paused combing my hair, resting the brush against the top of my head. My stomach twisted at the memory, and I started to breathe faster. "Take a couple of deep breaths, Lanny."

"I left Lio to look at the ocean just for a minute. And three boys followed me," I recounted, my mind racing and bile rising in my throat. "One of the boys...violated me."

The comb clattered to the floor.

"Oh my god," said Tiana, her voice shaking. "Baby, why didn't you tell me?"

Tears flowed from my eyes as she hugged me from behind, kissing my hair. She also had tears running down her face.

"I was so scared," I shuddered, looking at my hands as my tears flowed. "That's why I ran away, Mama. I didn't want to tell anyone, and our family is always so happy."

It felt like the weight of the world had been lifted from my shoulders after my confession. I felt lighter, freer, and the hidden resentment between us vanished. My mom was hurt when I ran away from home, and I felt it every day in my heart, but I couldn't address it.

Until now.

"I'm so sorry," said my mom, simply holding me with her arms around my neck and her cheek pressed to mine as we looked in the mirror. "I knew you weren't okay before you left. I heard you crying in your room for nights on end, and I felt so hopeless. I thought it would help for you to be around Grandma. I love you so much."

"I know, Mama. I'm just so happy to be marrying the best guys in the world today," I sighed.

"I couldn't wish for better," she agreed. "I just want to see you happy. And if these are the men you trust, I support you one hundred percent. I can't believe you carried this secret for so many years."

"I couldn't say anything," I said. "Grandma told me how you truly met my dads."

"I'm not surprised she told you," said Tiana, sounding annoyed. "Considering how much time you two spend together. I fell in love with your father, Grant since the moment I saw him. I was lucky in that, and I don't regret any moment with him."

"Well, Grandma made it sound much worse," I said.

"You know how she is," my mom winked, and we laughed together. She gave me one more kiss on my cheek. "Let's get you ready on your big day, okay? I want you to be happy and excited now."

"Okay," I said smiling, my heart light.

Lio

"Man, today's the day," said Markus excitedly, wringing his hands as we sat in the limo provided by the Royal Pack. "We're going to finally make it official."

"Hell yes," I said, straightening the red rose on my suit jacket. We all wore matching roses pinned to our black suits. My heart thumped at the thought of seeing Alana again, but this time in her wedding dress, marrying us.

"Hopefully, James can arrive in time to the palace," said Owen. "I don't know why he didn't want to ride with us."

King Armon offered to host our wedding to support us and to show the entire island that the vampires were welcome. The crimes against the vampires were escalating as the people tried destroying their startup businesses or not buying from them at all. I thought it was a smart move on the king's part to stop some of the hate.

"He'll be there," I reassured Owen. We had all gotten used to James flitting in and out of the house. As a leader of his people, he was busy managing things with his people and giving speeches. I wasn't sure exactly what the hell he did, but all I knew was that it would be better if he spent more time with Alana. She was happier and more excited when we were all together. "Shit, look at all the people."

There was a crowd in front of the palace grounds, blocked by a red rope to hold them back. There were a shit ton of delta guards, cops, and reporters everywhere. Cameras immediately turned to our limo as we parked in front of the pathway to the entrance.

"Fuck," said Markus. "I can't wait until all this is over and consummate our marriage to Alana."

"I know, right," said Owen in a low voice. He despised crowds.

"Guys, we got this," I said, rolling my neck and cracking my knuckles. I saw King Armon step out of his palace wearing regal red robes lined with gold. His wife, Queen Ophelia, stood beside him with a smile. "Let's marry our omega."

We got out of the limo, and the loud snapping of the cameras surrounded us on all sides. The crowd cheered, and Markus pumped his fist into the air. I smiled. Markus looked like he enjoyed the attention. I scanned the crowd for James and couldn't see him.

Fuck. *He needed to be here now.*

Our fiance would be walking down the aisle soon, and I wanted to make sure we were all at the altar, waiting and ready for our future bride. I walked towards King Armon with my pack following close behind me. I was thankful the crowd wasn't rowdy or hateful when they saw us. For months the news depicted us as sympathizers to the vampires and traitors. There was an entire hate campaign directed at the vampires. I rarely saw a vampire strolling on the street, in the shops, or even outside in general. They were still hiding and afraid of being staked by the common people on the island.

"Today's the big day!" boomed King Armon, shaking my hand, and I smiled widely. "Ready to marry your omega today?"

"I'm more than ready," I said as we stood at the entrance.

"Where's the vampire?" asked Armon.

"James. He'll be here soon," I said, turning my head back at the crowd and shading my eyes to see. Just as I said it, loud drumming sounded in the distance. I squinted my eyes to see what the hell was happening.

The crowd cleared a pathway to the new arrival, and I saw James arriving with an entourage of his people.

They were dressed in all different colors, festive and beating drums as they followed behind him. Their skin was translucent in the sun, and they had big smiles on their faces that showed off their fangs. He had brought his vampires with him and was being carried on a large throne-looking chair. I smiled, shaking my head.

He grinned widely when he saw me. Our professional photographer was going nuts, taking pictures from every angle.

"Shit, he went all out," muttered Owen in awe as we watched the vampires set his chair down at the front of the crowd. James wore a suit to match ours with a small black rose pinned to his blazer.

When James reached us, we greeted each other with brotherly hugs and slaps on the back.

"Damn James. I'm not going to forget this," said Markus, looking unbelievingly at the crowd of the colorful-looking vampires mixed in with the people.

"Now that we're all here," said King Armon. "Let us go inside now."

The room where we would have our ceremony was already filled with our guests. The palace was decked out today, especially the room we would be marrying in. Towering marble columns adorned with delicate carvings led to a majestic arched doorway. There was lavish seating adorned with purple plush cushions and matching purple flowers entwined with vines hanging down the walls. Large chandeliers hung from the ceiling, which cast a warm glow to the room.

We passed by my fathers, who were pleased that I quit my professional knotting job. My father, Jatix, had never been happy with it and called Alana a blessing in my life. I noticed Markus's father was there, who was already half-asleep in his chair and scratching his mustache.

Owen's parents, Annie and Tom, were excitedly perched on the edge of their seats, smiling as they gazed at us.

We assembled at the front of the altar.

I was eager to finally see her. My eyes were on the aisle, waiting for the bride of my dreams to appear in all her beauty and grace. I knew the rest of the men felt the same. All of us were filled with jittery nerves. She would be arriving soon.

The music started playing, and I took deep breaths as my stomach twisted in knots.

"Fuck, I don't know what to do," said Owen.

"Relax," I whispered. "Take deep breaths and just focus on her. Lana's going to be our wife very soon, and we need to show the strength that she can trust us with her life."

I had to take my own advice as I waited for her to appear, taking deep breaths.

The world around me seemed to fade away, leaving only the soft melody of the wedding march echoing in my ears. My eyes were locked on the grand hall entrance, where she would soon appear, my beautiful bride. I couldn't help but feel a mix of nerves and excitement, eager to catch the first glimpse of her.

As the doors swung open, her maids of honor, Alana's sisters, walked in first, and my heart was beating in anticipation. Roxanne and Sarah wore matching shimmering pink dresses, carrying small pink bouquets.

Then I saw my bride, and my heart stopped.

Alana was breathtaking as she walked, clutching her father Grant's elbow. She was a vision wearing all white, her gown flowed gracefully with every movement, and the delicate lace adorned her like a regal queen. The veil framed her face, but her eyes shone through with a sparkle that was uniquely Alana's. Her eyes locked with mine, and I felt the warmth of tears forming in my eyes. The joy and pride I felt in this moment was immeasurable. I couldn't help but think how lucky and blessed I was to have her as my omega, my confidante, my love.

This woman would be officially ours from this day forward.

Time slowed as we held each other's gaze, silently reaffirming our commitment to each other and the life we would build together.

Alana

Oh, my heart.

I took a deep breath, trying to steady the rapid flutter of my heart.

I couldn't believe it when I was finally standing before my four mates at the altar, and my eyes darted nervously between them. They were all strong and confident in their own right, and I was about to marry them all.

Doubts and worries ran through my mind. *What if I couldn't be everything they needed? What if I couldn't keep them all happy?* My hands trembled slightly, clutching the bouquet tightly as if seeking comfort.

The weight of their gaze on me felt both overwhelming and comforting. They all wore gentle smiles, a mixture of understanding and support in their eyes. They knew how anxious I was and were here to reassure me, just as they always had been. I could hear the whispers among the guests, a mixture of curiosity and judgment. This was uncharted territory, and not everyone could comprehend the depth of our connection.

I was marrying two alphas, a beta, and a vampire. The unlikeliest connection of them all.

"Welcome," the officiant said, his voice resonating through the halls- booming and clear. "Ladies and gentlemen- today we are here to witness the union between Alana Frostcrown and her four dedicated mates. Today, they pledge to support and cherish one another, to love and care for each other."

My heart raced as he asked Lio, Markus, Owen, and James if they would marry me.

With each resounding yes, my heart grew bigger, and tears pricked my eyes. *Don't cry, Alana. Don't cry.* The officiant then turned to me.

"Do you, Alana Frostcrown, accept Lionel, Markus, James, and Owen to be your lawfully wedded husbands?"

"I do," I said, my lips trembling with emotion.

"By the power vested in me, I now pronounce you joined in this extraordinary bond of love. You may now seal your union with a kiss."

With a nod from the officiant, all four males stepped forward, grasping my veil from the edge of it at the same time, lifting it gently over my head. As the sheer fabric was lifted away, I could see the warmth in their eyes, a reflection of their love for me. My breath caught in my throat, and I couldn't help but admire how they looked at me as if I were the center of their universe.

Lio, ever the protector, leaned in first, his touch reassuring. His lips brushed against mine in the sweetest kiss, and it felt like coming home. It was the most loving and touching kiss he'd ever given me, and I could feel the emotion behind it as we pulled away. His eyes were teary, and the look in his eyes conveyed to me that I was the one for him.

Markus, the most dominant alpha I've ever met, kissed me next, his thick beard brushing my face. His lips pressed against mine, and he would've stuck his tongue in my mouth if I didn't pull away. He winked at me when the kiss ended, and I blushed.

James, my most unexpected connection, leaned in next with excitement in his eyes. "My wife." Then he kissed me tenderly, cupping my chin with two fingers, lifting my face to him. My heart was racing fast. I was married to the leader of the vampires now. When we pulled away, I smiled shyly at him, and he grinned.

Owen kissed me last. His kiss was filled with passion and a sense of shared excitement for our journey ahead. I knew he was excited by how his eyes gleamed when our kiss ended. The guests erupted into cheers and applause, celebrating our unity.

In this moment, it felt like it was just the five of us in the world, cocooned in a bubble of love and happiness.

With my hands intertwined between James and Lio, we turned to face the people.

"We're married now," I said so that only my mates could hear amongst the cheers of the crowd.

"Yes, we are, my love," said James, and Lio squeezed my hand on my other side. My heart was full of love at this moment, more than I'd ever felt before. I was a married omega now, and tonight would be the marking between us. My heart beat fast again at the thought, and I couldn't wait.

Later that day, the reception party the palace held for us was spectacular. The ballroom was filled with twinkling fairy lights and vibrant floral arrangements. I danced with each mate in turn on the marble floors, which glowed under our feet.

Markus held me in his arms as we danced around the ballroom. The chandeliers lit up the room, and everything felt magical as he spun me, holding me close to his warm body. We danced to Lacy singing on the stage. She was Vanessa's daughter and was pretty much a recluse after starting her singing career. We weren't that close because of our different paths in life, but we did grow up together along with Lio.

"I didn't know you could dance," I said as Markus caught me after dipping me in his arms.

"I'm full of surprises," he growled, and I giggled. "When you giggle like that...I might rut you right here in front of everyone."

"Oh no," I said, sobering instantly, so he didn't do exactly that. With Markus, it was unpredictable. He could take me at any time, and I couldn't refuse him. His muscular arms surrounding me in his body heat were already making me horny enough as it was. I looked at the guests, noticing Markus's father as he walked towards us with a drink in his hand. He looked tipsy already, but we ended our dance and turned to him.

"Congratulations, son," he said gruffly, giving Markus a one-armed hug.

"Thanks, Dad," said Markus, his cheeks red with embarrassment. I smiled to show that it didn't affect me one bit. I enjoyed hanging out with Markus's father. During the year that I was engaged to the pack, I met all of their families.

"Alana, my daughter-in-law," he roared, lifting his drink in the air, and everyone clapped. It was my turn to blush, and I was relieved when someone took him away, gently leading him to a seat.

Markus and I walked to the rest of the pack at the table on the stage. I had danced with all the men already, and it was time we had a bite to eat. On our way to the stage, I kissed my baby twins, who Sarah and Adam were watching now. Jay was on Adam's lap as Adam fed him spoonfuls of rice. My sister Sarah was holding June as they watched people dancing. My mother was dancing with her husbands, and June was clapping wildly as she watched them with slobber dripping down her chin.

"Sarah," I said, hugging her and June. "Thank you for taking care of the babies."

"Anytime, sis," said Sarah, looking at me with kohl-rimmed eyes. "You looked stunning all day, by the way."

"I try," I said sarcastically, flipping my hair back in mock arrogance, and she laughed.

"Hey, aren't you going to thank me, too?" said Adam, and I rolled my eyes.

"Umm, Sarah and Roxy are always taking care of the babies," I said. "This is literally the first time you're pitching in."

"Lies," said Adam, smiling. "I've been working hard."

"Jay will remember it forever though," I warned, and Adam gave Jay a peck on the cheek. Adam wasn't one for affection, and I wondered how the hell he would cope with an omega in his future.

After the reception, we left the palace with a huge procession behind us. The guests cheered and clapped, throwing rice and petals at us.

James opened the door to the limo, and I smiled gratefully.

I pulled myself into the limo, dragging my huge wedding dress inside.

I chuckled at myself with how much space I took up with my overflowing dress and veil. It was so hot. I couldn't wait to fling off all my clothes and cool off.

My husbands got in after me, and I was sandwiched between Owen and Lio. Markus and James sat across from us. I waved at my family through the tinted window, wondering if they could see me. I could hear the cheers of everyone, music, and celebration as our limo drove off into the night.

Owen laid his hand on my thigh and kissed my cheek.

"That was quite the wedding. Best wedding I've ever been to," he said.

"Oh yes," I laughed, leaning against his chest. Lio rubbed my back, and I closed my eyes to rest for a second. All the males' attention was focused on me, and I could already guess their dirty thoughts for our wedding night. My heart pounded in anticipation of what they had planned. While my eyes were closed, I could feel Lio lifting my wedding dress over my legs and my thighs. "What?! Should we wait until we reach our destination?"

"We just want a sneak peek of what's to come," he said gruffly, and my heart pounded. My privates started to throb as he hiked my dress higher, and I opened my eyes with my head still on Owen's chest.

Lio pulled me onto his lap, and I yelped in surprise.

"Damn," said Owen, watching Lio spread my legs on his lap while my back was pressed against his chest. He spread my legs over the outside of his knees with my dress hiked up all the way, showing off

243

my white thong to the men.

"Oh hell," said Markus, his gaze glued to my pussy.

James leaned back and touched his dick over his pants. "Her white panties are dark and wet."

"Take a nice look before we fuck her tonight," said Lio, spreading my legs further, trapping me open with his knees. God, he was the expert at foreplay, making me excited for my wedding night. I gripped Lio's forearms to try and stop his hand from going between my legs.

"Let's wait until we're inside somewhere," I protested. "The driver is probably listening."

"I don't give a fuck what the driver thinks," Lio growled in my ear, which sent pleasant shivers through my body. His fingers dipped between my legs, pulling my thong to the side until my pussy was exposed to all of them.

"Fuck," said Owen. "She's already nice and dripping for all our cocks."

"Put your finger inside her," James requested.

"My pleasure," said Lio, and I gasped when he plunged his thick middle finger into my pussy, already drenched with slick. It was embarrassing being outed that I was already horny for our wedding night, but inside, I was giddy. "I'll leave my finger inside her the entire ride, but first, I need to plug her little ass."

"What?!" I gasped, surprised.

We hardly ever used toys. My eyes widened when James handed him a small bullet-shaped plug like this had been planned in advance. Lio removed his finger from my pussy and grabbed the anal plug. His little finger slipped down my ass cheeks.

"Hold her open, Owen," Lio commanded, and Owen was quick to

obey. I looked down shyly as Markus and James stared at my privates being on display. I knew I should be used to it by now.

But hell, each time it happened, I couldn't stop my nervousness from taking over.

"Mhm," said Owen, gripping my ass cheeks open. A rush of air hit my privates, and I bit my lip. "Our little omega is blushing."

"I can't wait to fucking make her pregnant tonight," growled Markus as he touched himself, watching me.

I gripped Lio's arm again as he gently swirled the tip of the plug against my anus, pushing it in as he did so. I gasped at the fullness. It was in all the way now, and Lio groaned in delight. I could feel his cock bouncing under my butt in excitement. He was hard as stone, and I knew he was ready to fuck me tonight.

"Good girl," Owen praised, releasing my ass cheeks and closing it around the heavy plug inside me. The weight of the plug turned me on immensely, and I craved their cocks inside me. Lio then pressed his finger back into my pussy, making me aroused and frustrated for the rest of the ride.

When the limo stopped moving, Lio removed his finger from my now-sopping pussy. He pulled my dress down and lifted me out of the limo. With my legs closed, it was hard to ignore the plug in my asshole. It jiggled inside me with every step.

Once we were outside, I was confused. There wasn't a building around for miles.

"Where are we?" I asked.

245

"It's a surprise," said Lio smiling. I was getting scared. We were in the middle of the wilderness, the beach not too far from us. "We just have to walk a little bit."

"Okay, I trust you," I said, laying my head against his arm as he carried me. "I can walk. Especially if it's a long..."

"No," said Lio sharply. "You are our bride, and we're more than capable of carrying you."

"Spoken like a true alpha," said Owen sheepishly, and I giggled.

"Close your eyes," said Lio, and I did. I could hear my husbands' footsteps crunching on the leaves and their murmurs while the ocean waves sounded in the distance. Markus and James argued about sports and which pack did a better job. While they talked, I could feel myself start to drift into sleep. After a few minutes, Lio stopped walking and gently set me down on the ground. "Don't open your eyes yet."

"I almost fell asleep," I groaned.

"It's only nine," said Owen as he took my other hand, guiding me to the surprise they set up for me.

"Okay, open your eyes."

I opened my eyes to see a massive tent lit with orange lights inside. I gasped when I saw the little fairy lights surrounding the outside of the tent, hanging from giant poles. The entrance of the tent was open to reveal a luxurious white mattress inside and a small table of refreshments. A campfire was next to the tent, a large fire roaring between a bed of rocks.

"It's so beautiful," I said, tears flowing down my face. "This is so crazy, oh my god."

"For you, sweetheart," said Lio. "I thought we could roast some marshmallows and relax a bit before our wedding night?"

We looked at each other, remembering the magical night we had together when we were just teens. The night that was ultimately destroyed for me. I wanted to cry at this gesture of his.

"Why a campfire?" I asked.

"For you to have new memories with me at a campfire," he chuckled. "Why are you crying my sweet?"

I sniffled and tried to brush my tears away, but he was already kissing my tears away.

"I can't believe you did this for me."

"You're worth the world," said James. "We came up with this idea, because we knew how horrible that night was for you. We're going to change your memories tonight. Will you join us for some roasted marshmallows?"

"I would love to," I said, my heart bursting with joy.

As we sat around the campfire, I was getting antsy with the plug inside my ass. I wanted something bigger, and every time I walked, it would tug at my privates, reminding me that it was my wedding night. James fed me a bite from his roasted marshmallow which was sweet and sticky on my tongue.

"Eat the whole thing, baby," said James. "I don't get how you like this sweet stuff. It tastes like fucking paper."

I bit off the entire marshmallow closing my eyes in pleasure.

"It's because you like blood," I said, and James chuckled darkly. Lio leaned in towards me and kissed my sticky lips. When he pulled back, he licked his lips with desire in his eyes. Owen was relaxing in the tent already, and I could see the shadow of his feet kicked up on the couch inside it.

"King Armon asked where we would be staying for our wedding

247

night," said Lio.

"So you told him to do this?" I asked incredulously.

"Yep," said Markus.

"I can't believe he'd do all this for us," I said.

"He's probably feeling guilty after how we were treated," said James, tracing my arm with a finger. His touch made goosebumps rise on my skin. His finger traced all the way up my arm and to my lips. "How about we undress our bride now?"

"Sounds like a good idea," agreed Lio.

"I'll carry her," said Markus, quickly scooping me up in his big strong arms.

"Eek," I said. "I hope I'm not too heavy."

"Don't ever say that again," said Markus, kissing me on the lips and full of hard desire.

The tent had an air conditioner which I was grateful for as I lay in the bed between my husbands. The bed was extra large and fit us all, which I loved. I was lying naked in the middle of all of them, each husband surrounding me as we took a moment to relax after the hectic wedding.

"You are protected by the circle of your pack," said Lio.

"We are one," said Markus, and my heart pounded fast. *Were they going to mark me right now?* I wasn't sure how any of this worked, and omegas were shy to say what happened between their packs.

"What if someone sees us?" I asked worriedly, looking at the tent entrance. "Or if they come in."

"If anyone dares walk in..." growled Lio.

"Dead on sight," said James in an equally terrifying voice. A blush rose in my cheeks, and my heart pounded faster at their fierce protectiveness of me.

"Oh, okay," I squeaked. "I guess I'm safe then."

"You're very safe in here with us," said James.

"Except that all of our cocks are fucking hard for our new bride," said Markus.

"We will take her by two tonight. Someone in her ass, and someone will take her pussy," said Lio, massaging my breasts, and I moaned in delight. "Owen, you're already on top of her. How about you take her pussy? Who wants to take her in the ass?"

"Me," said James quickly, and my face turned hot.

"I would love to take her pussy," Owen breathed as he kissed me on the lips.

"We will watch and witness the consummation," said Lio.

"Perfect," said Owen. "I'm more than fucking ready to make her ours."

My heart skipped a beat at his statement.

"I agree," said James, who made his way to my backside. Markus and Lio moved to the far side of the bed, watching as I was about to get taken by Owen and James. Owen started to play with my clit with his thumb.

"I'm already horny, don't worry," I breathed, but Owen cut me off with another kiss on my lips as he rubbed my pussy around in circles. When I felt my belly tightening with arousal, he aligned his cock to my pussy.

"I want you to feel every pleasure imaginable," said Owen, plunging into my very wet pussy. I arched my hips eagerly to his, matching his lovemaking as he rocked into me. His thick cock stretched my pussy as he thrust into me.

I could feel James twisting the anal plug and popping it out of my anus. My holes clenched at the wonderful sensation, pulling a moan from my lips. I felt all the sensations as they played with my body.

Markus cupped and squeezed my breasts from above. Every inch of me was being touched, kissed, or licked. James replaced the plug with his cock, stretching my ass. I threw my head back as I felt Owen's and James's cocks pounding into me.

I felt James's cold breath on my shoulder from behind as we lay on our side.

"I'm going to feed from you," said James, and my heart thumped in delight. "Consider this my official mating mark."

His fangs bit into the side of my neck, and I yelped. He licked the wound, erasing the stinging pain before he started to suck on my blood. I moaned, dropping my head onto the pillow as I looked into Owen's eyes.

Owen kissed my lips as he pistoned into me. His tongue pressed into my mouth, and I swirled my tongue with his. Markus's finger rubbed my clit, and my belly tightened with familiar arousal while James and Owen plunged inside me.

"Do you feel that beta fucking you?" James whispered in my ear. "He wants to cum inside you so bad."

At his words, my belly tightened even more. The tightness snapped as I moaned through my powerful orgasm. Owen yelled as his cock exploded inside me, with my pussy clenched around his cock. He collapsed next to me, spent and breathing hard as he caressed my hair in wonder.

"Fuck," said Owen, kissing gently on the lips. "We've consummated the marriage, my bride."

But James wasn't done. He flipped me onto my belly, and my face was pressed against the pillow as he fucked me from behind. My pussy was throbbing from my orgasm, but this felt so fucking hot.

I wanted it all.

He gripped my hips powerfully as he pounded into my ass from behind, with my legs spread as wide as possible for him.

"Damn," I heard Markus muttering behind me as he watched James take full control of my body.

"Your asshole needs my dick," grunted James, and I cried out when he plunged one last time to the hilt. The thickness of his cold cock stretching my asshole like never before had me shocked in place. I hadn't had a good knotting in my ass in a while. Then I felt his cum spurt into my asshole, gushing down the back of my thighs. "Good girl."

James laid on top of me as we caught our breath. This was the wildest night I've ever had with the pack and the hottest.

"We'll allow you to rest for a couple of minutes before Markus and I take you next," said Lio as I lay underneath James, basking in the coolness of his body. It was getting hot and sweaty in the tent after I was fucked in the middle of two males. Owen fed me a few grapes as I tried to recover, twisting my head to the side of the pillow.

"I love you," said James, kissing the back of my head. He slowly retracted his cock from my ass and walked to the snack table.

I turned over to my side while Owen fed me more of the juicy grapes. Lio took his place behind me.

"Such a thick juicy butt," said Lio, gripping my ass cheeks and smacking me. I giggled as I chewed on the last of the grapes from Owen's hands. "I don't know how we got so lucky to be with such a curvy omega like yourself."

I placed my hand over my chubby belly, lined with stretch marks. Owen removed my hand.

"Don't be shy, babe," he said. "We adore every inch of you. Stretch marks and all. I'm sure I'm speaking for every alpha and vampire in the room."

"Hear, hear," said James in agreement, drinking a swig of wine from the refreshments. "I can't bring myself to walk away from her. Not for a moment, and I'm considering giving my leadership over to Volgriff's brother."

"What?" I asked, shocked. I've been wanting James to spend more time with me for the past year.

"Yes," said James. "I want to be with you fully, little omega."

I blushed, and my heart glowed as he gazed at me over his glass.

After I was relaxed again, Owen moved over to the edge of the mattress so Markus could take his spot in front of me. Lio was rubbing his hand down my sides, warming me up for the knotting that would happen now.

My heart raced at the thought.

"I'll take your tight little ass this time," Lio muttered in my ear from behind. "Markus will be delighted to impregnate you tonight. Isn't that right, Mark?"

"Yes, sir," said Markus, his eyes on my pussy. "Spread her."

Lio lifted my leg from behind, hooking my leg behind his knee. I felt his hard cock press against my already stretched ass. My ass wasn't stretched enough for a knotting, though and my stomach clenched in anticipation.

Markus fingered my pussy, swirling around Owen's liquids with mine. His pointer finger rubbed my clit as he brought his body closer to mine. I felt his hairy thigh press against me as Lio lifted his knee, spreading my right leg upwards. Markus's heavy, pierced cock, hung in front of my pussy as I watched him bring it closer to me. He rubbed the tip of his thick cock against my pussy, and I felt his piercing rubbing gently against my clit.

Arousal strummed through my body as he did that.

"Please put it inside me," I begged, unable to take the tension anymore.

Lio was slowly inserting his cock between my ass cheeks while I was focused on Markus. I yelped when I felt Lio's cock plunge into my anus.

"There you go," said Lio soothingly, rubbing my shoulders. "You took my cock inside your ass very well."

I felt my ass stretching and getting used to Lio's member as he pushed deeper inside me. Markus inserted his cock halfway into my pussy, and I groaned with pleasure as he stretched me with every inch.

Markus's cock was still huge to me. He was always a surprise every time he fucked me.

"Fuck yes," Markus growled when he pressed the enormity of his cock inside me. "Do you like that, sweetheart?"

"Yes," I gasped. Both alphas' cocks inside me had me stretched to the limit. The last time they fucked me at the same time was at the heat clinic.

"At the same time. Ready?" said Lio, and Markus nodded silently.

"Oh," I gasped when their cocks pushed up inside me at the same time. They pulled back simultaneously and thrust back into me. "Oh god." Markus and Lio were relentless on our wedding night. They continued to thrust into me in perfect rhythm, which only heightened the feeling for me.

"We will mark her at the same time as we rut," ordered Lio. I felt Lio's lips on my collarbone from behind, and Markus pressed his lips on my neck, opposite of where James marked me.

My heart pounded faster, scared it would hurt at the same time.

When they both bit into me, I screamed as the sharp pain hit me and radiated down to the core of my belly.

"*Mine*," growled Lio.

"*Mate*," said Markus, purring into me to ease my pain.

My stomach clenched powerfully, and I released a gush of slick from my pussy and anus. They quickly licked my wounds, easing the sharp pain as they continued to thrust into me. Soon after, I heard Lio growl behind me, his hot breath washing over my ear as he climaxed into my ass. Markus roared loudly as his cock swelled inside my pussy.

Both cocks swelling inside me made me gasp. It had been awhile.

"The marking and rutting of our omega is complete," said Lio. "No other pack will come near her. No one will ever hurt our precious Alana."

I lay spent between the two alphas, breathing hard with my breasts pressed against Markus's hard chest and knotted on both ends. I never felt safer as I did now after being mated and marked by my pack.

"I love you all," I said, as contentment washed over every fiber of my being. "This was the best day and night ever."

"I love you too, Alana," said Markus, kissing me on the lips tenderly.

I felt Lio's kiss on my shoulder, his chest hard against my back. He whispered, "I love you like I've never loved anyone before in my life. You're my one and only. You're our wife and our treasure."

James came around to the top of my head and kissed me while I was knotted to the two alphas. I looked up at him and smiled after his lips left mine.

"Never in a million years did I think I'd join a pack of werewolves," he said to me. "I never thought I'd marry after what happened to my family. You are the light of my life and the hope in my soul, even through my darkest moments. I love you, little omega."

"I love you too," I whispered as the glow in my heart grew stronger for each of them. "I knew you were my fated mate since the moment I saw you and searched for you all those years. Ever since you saved me from a pack of strangers."

"I would save you in a heartbeat. But next time, no survivors," said James, kissing me again.

Owen kissed each of my toes, and I giggled at the sensation.

"I love you too, missy," he said. "After these alphas un-knot from you, it'll be bathtime in the ocean. Just the two of us."

"You greedy bastard," said Markus, and we all burst into laughter.

I never felt happier in this moment shared with my forever pack.

A blissful sigh escaped my lips as contentment washed over me. In the safety of their love, I knew nothing would ever hurt me. Ever again. I had never felt so protected, loved, and adored like this in my life. And so, as we lay there entangled in each other's embrace, I cherished the beautiful aftermath of our passion and the unbreakable bond between my alphas, beta, and a vampire in my bed.

THE END

Continue reading on to **Book 7**: **Craved by The Pack** featuring Lacy (Vanessa's daughter). *A beautiful omega singer stalked by alphas and forced to hire five hot AF bodyguards. Will she ever find true love with a pack?*
If you haven't read Vanessa's story yet, read it here! Betrayed by The Pack

Author's Note

Thank you so much for reading!

Thank you so much for reading *Knotted by The Pack*. I really hope you enjoyed it! If you've made it this far, I'd appreciate it if you left a review on Amazon, letting me know what you think! It helps authors like me keep building stories for you to enjoy for a long time to come.

Please let me know what you'd like to see more from me and the hottest scenes you like from the book. You can include your feedback, and all fan mail can go to: author_laylasparks@yahoo.com

Follow me on social media for sneak peeks of new stories, and watch your favorite scenes from the series!

Subscribe to my Newsletter

Tiktok: @laylasparks_author

Instagram: https://www.instagram.com/author_laylasparks/

Twitter: https://twitter.com/LaylaSparks7

Also By Layla Sparks

Howl's Edge Island: Omega For The Pack Series (Reverse Harem Series)

Book 1 (*Tiana's story*): Stolen by The Pack

Book 2 (*Keera's story*): Auctioned to the Pack

Book 3 (*Lyra's story*): Princess For The Pack

Book 4 (*Vanessa's story*): Betrayed by The Pack

Book 5 (*Jade's story*): Matched to The Pack

Book 6 (*Alana's story*): Knotted by The Pack

Book 7 (*Lacy's story*): Craved by The Pack

Captive After Moonlight Series: DARK Romance Erotica

Jenna gets a lot more than she can handle when visiting the smutty toy shop downtown. She looks for the perfect naughty toy, but little does she know that a werewolf is looking for *his* toy...

Now she's kidnapped by a psycho HOT werewolf who believes Jenna should be his.

Book 1: Werewolf's Mate

Book 2: Werewolf's Captive

Five Sexy Bigfoot Short Stories: Kink For Monsters Erotica

Book: Five Sexy Bigfoot Short Stories

Alien Erotica Series: Tantalizing Tentacles of Korynz: (Kidnapping & Age Gap Erotica)

Book 1: Disciplined by My Alien Teacher

Book 2: Examined by My Alien Doctor

Book 3: Enslaved by The Alien King

-On Kindle Unlimited

Printed in Great Britain
by Amazon